MW01706857

A Gift from
Gio

CECE BELL

Color by David Lasky

AMULET BOOKS
NEW YORK

El Deafo

Library of Congress Control Number: 2013955590

Paperback ISBN: 978-1-4197-1217-3
Hardcover ISBN: 978-1-4197-1020-9

Text and illustrations copyright © 2014 Cece Bell

Color by David Lasky
Book design by Cece Bell and Kate Fitch

The Phonic Ear is the registered trademark of
William Dernant Holding A/S. Used by permission.

Published in 2014 by Amulet Books, an imprint of ABRAMS. All rights reserved. No portion of this book may be reproduced, stored in a retrieval system, or transmitted in any form or by any means, mechanical, electronic, photocopying, recording, or otherwise, without written permission from the publisher.

Amulet Books and Amulet Paperbacks are registered
trademarks of Harry N. Abrams, Inc.

Printed and bound in China
10 9 8

Amulet Books are available at special discounts when purchased in quantity for premiums and promotions as well as fundraising or educational use. Special editions can also be created to specification. For details, contact specialsales@abramsbooks.com or the address below.

ABRAMS
THE ART OF BOOKS SINCE 1949
115 West 18th Street
New York, NY 10011
www.abramsbooks.com

one

I was a regular little kid. I played with my mom's stuff.
I watched TV with my big brother, Ashley, and my big sister, Sarah.
♪BatMAN!♫
I rode on the back of my father's bicycle.
WHEEEEEEEEEEEE!
I found caterpillars with my friend Emma.
And I sang.
WE ALL LIVE IN A YELLOW SUBMARINE, A YELLOW SUBMARINE—

But then everything changed.
—A YELLOW SUBMARINE...
CECE?
GEORGE! DO SOMETHING! HURRY!
My parents rush me to the hospital.
PLEASE HURRY
MISS THE TURN OH SHE
MUCH WORSE PLEASE
GOD IN
HAPPEN TO
THE

PLEASE HELP US— SHE'S SO SICK!
I am pulled away from my parents...
...and taken to a room. Somebody sticks a needle in my back.
THE FLUID FROM HER SPINE TELLS US SHE HAS MENINGITIS. HER BRAIN MIGHT SWELL—
BUT SHE'S ONLY *FOUR!*

I wake up. I'm in a different room.
ONLY
A doctor comes...
WE NEED TO MEASURE YOUR HEAD!
...and a nurse comes...
THIS WON'T HURT A BIT!
...and oh, but my head hurts. Really bad!

The arm prickings and head measurings are endless! It looks like I'll be here for a while.
But after many days of treatment, I am well enough to share a room with another sick kid.
Something is *different*, though. But *what*? I can't quite figure it out.
CECE. *CECE!* WANT SOME ICE CREAM?
HUH—I GUESS SHE DOESN'T WANT ANY...
For one thing, how come I never get any ice cream? The other kid gets it all the time!
!

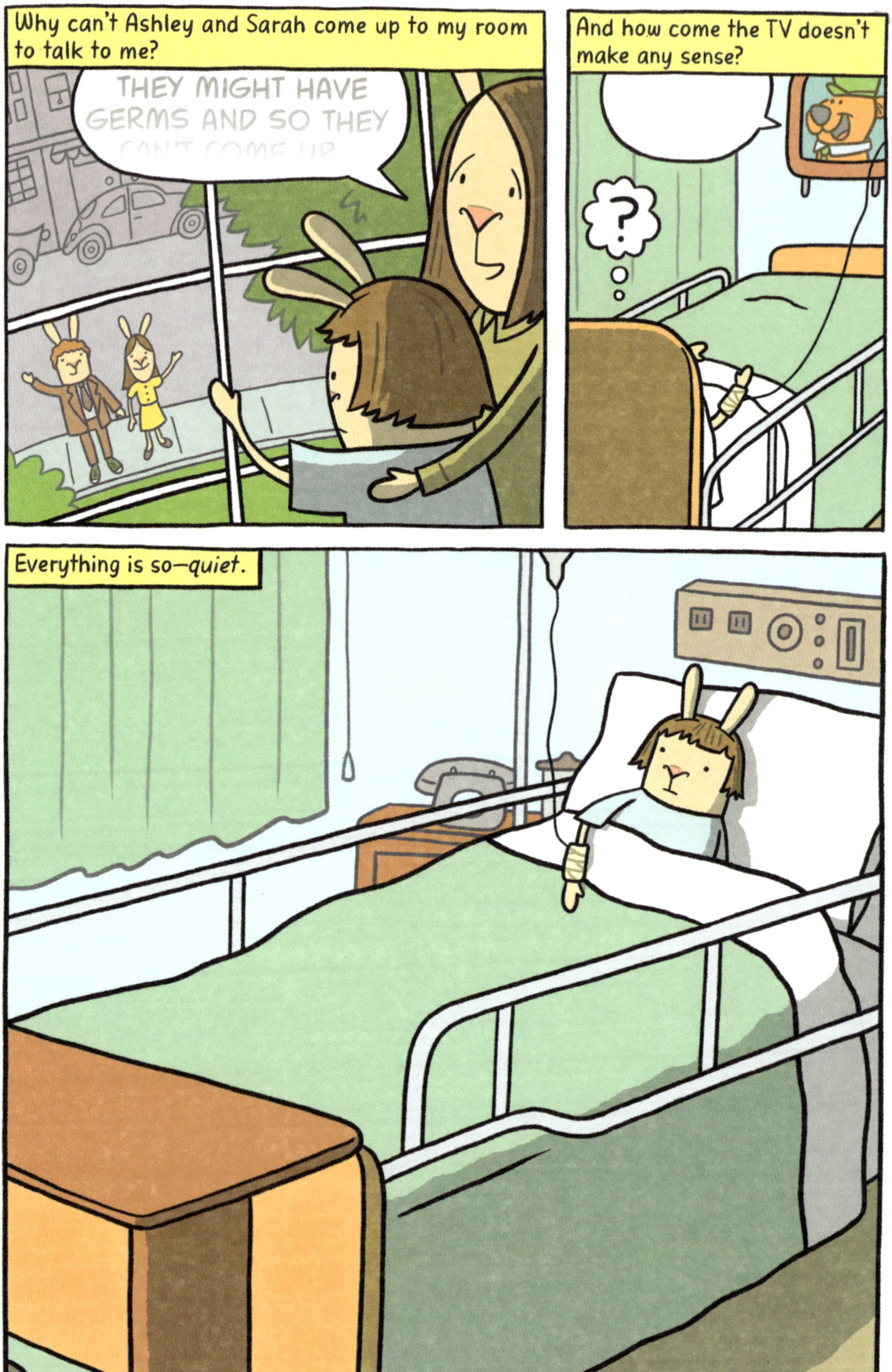
Why can't Ashley and Sarah come up to my room to talk to me?
THEY MIGHT HAVE GERMS AND SO THEY CAN'T COME UP
And how come the TV doesn't make any sense?
?
Everything is so—*quiet*.

It's not *all* bad, though. I get lots of great gifts!
THE MEANEST SQUIRREL I EVER MET
To: Cece
From: the Collins
by GENE ZION
pictures by MARGARET BLOY GRAHAM
LOVE EMMA
And I start to feel better. I put on one of the gifts. It's time to get up!
But I can't stand up—

I can't even walk!
I can crawl, though. And after a few days of practice, I regain my balance.
I'm feeling so much better!

I think I might even be *all* better!
Finally—*finally!*—I get to leave the hospital...
...and go home.

Miracle of miracles, my siblings are being nice to me!
Ashley has made and hidden hundreds of paper boats all around the house just for me...
...and has filled each one with a special surprise.
CANDY!
And Sarah sits close to my bed at night...
...until I fall asleep.

I wake up every morning happy and relieved to be home.
I stay close to Mama, no matter where she is.
But suddenly, I lose her.

Where is she?
I call out but she doesn't answer me!
When I finally find her, I know that everything is different. I think she knows it, too.
I CAN'T HEAR...

two

It's been two weeks since the hospital. Just because I can't hear good doesn't mean I can't *look* good.
I *love* my bathing suit.
I wear it—and nothing else—
every day, everywhere.
I LOOK *FANTASTIC!*

But today, it looks like I have to get "dressed."
I don't want to!
But I do.
WE MUST BE GOING SOMEWHERE "SPECIAL"!
One hour later, we're in the car. I wish I knew where we were going.
PLEASE DON'T BE THE HOSPITAL PLEASE PLEASE PLEASE...
AUDIOLOGY
WHEW! IT'S NOT THE HOSPITAL!
THAT MAN SURE LOOKS LIKE A DOCTOR TO ME!

The man who isn't a doctor but looks like one shows me a big bell...
...and then he puts a blindfold on me.
?

Then it gets *really* strange. The man puts headphones on my ears...
...and motions for me to go inside a booth.
I don't want to!
But I do.
An amazing thing happens inside the booth: I hear a beep! A real beep! It's the first sound I've heard since the hospital. And then I hear something that sounds sort of like talking, but it's all *weird*.
RAAY YOE HANN WAH OOO EER AAH BEEP!
HUH? *OH!* MAYBE HE SAID "RAISE YOUR HAND WHEN YOU HEAR A BEEP." I'LL TRY THAT...

BEEP
Booop
ooooop
BEEP!
And then we're done.
The man shows me and my parents a chart he has filled out. My parents don't seem too happy after that.
& HEARING CENTER, INC.
ROANOKE, VIRGINIA 24014
FREQUENCY IN HERTZ
Speech Audiometry
?

Then the man squirts some goop into each of my ears...
EW!
...and I wait...and I wait and wait...
...until the man pulls the firmed-up goop out of my ears.
And then we're done.
IS THAT A LOLLIPOP?
WHAT A STRANGE MAN! MMM, CHERRY! MY FAVORITE!

One week later...
AGAIN?
Today the man shows me a little box with cords attached to it.
!
He puts the little box in an ugly green pouch—and then he puts the little pouch on me.
He puts those funny-looking ear globs—the ones he made last week—back into my ears.
Then he pushes a button...
...and adjusts a dial—
EERS DEE HALOOM UNOLL, JUSS ACK ON AH EEHEE SET—ETT ILLY EEZEE! AH HINK ILL LAHK AYRIN ESS MODEL, ETT ONE UH DEE ESS AID HOUT THAR...

I CAN *HEAR!* BUT WHAT ARE THEY *SAYING?*

CAN. YOU. HEAR. ME?
I UNDERSTOOD THAT! WOW!
YES!
BUT HOW DOES IT LOOK?
UMMMM...
Luckily, the man gives me a beautiful pouch for the little box...
...and another lollipop. Gee, I can really hear! But will I *look* good, too?
I CAN HEAR MYSELF EATING THIS LOLLIPOP!

When I get home, I put my bathing suit back on, and I put the little box into the cute pouch.
I strap the whole thing on. I put the ear globs in my ears, and I look in the mirror.
Hmmm. Not great...but not bad, either.
THOSE CORDS, THOUGH!

three

I find out that the little box is called a "hearing aid." It's hard to get used to. Everything sounds funny when I use it. Even me!
EEEP. BOOP. OOP. EEEP? HELLO. HELLO? AH! AH!
I don't like the way my hearing aid looks, either, so I cover it up with some "real" clothes. I'm going to visit my friend Emma today. I haven't seen her since I got sick.
BUT HOW AM I GONNA HIDE THE CORDS? HMMM...
Emma and I have always looked different from each other, but in ways that didn't matter.
BOY! EMMA SURE IS A LOT TALLER THAN ME IN THIS PICTURE!
Emma & Cece, August 1974
Cece & Emma, February 1975

And *now*? Now we look a *lot* different, and in a way that *does* matter. To me, at least.
I THIG YOO LOO GOO!
HUH?
AH ZEDD, AH THIG YOO LOO GOOOO!
EH SOUNZ LAH YUR UNNAH WAWAH!
HEY! I DIDN'T KNOW YOU'D STILL BE ABLE TO TALK!
YOU SOUND A LITTLE *FUNNY*, THOUGH...
I TALK DIFFERENT, TOO? OH NO.

Simple conversations are now so difficult!
DOO YOO WAN SUMDING DO DRING? WE HAFF JERRY'S MOP...
Cherry POP
Cherry POP
Jerry
SHOES...
ORANGE JUICE
OR A GOAT!
MAAA!
Coca
I'LL HAVE THE GOAT!
Coca
HUH?

At the end of summer, it's time to start kindergarten. I now have definite proof that Emma and I are different: she gets on one bus...
...and I get on another.
I don't know where Emma goes, but I take a terrifying bus ride holding the hand of a mysterious woman with a serious afro.

The bus stops in front of what I think is my new school.
J.B. FISHER MODEL SCHOOL
The woman from the bus leads me down a hallway.
I JUST *KNOW* EVERYONE IS LOOKING AT ME!
We stop at a door. This must be my new classroom. I'm afraid to look up. But I do.
SHE'S GOT CORDS STICKING OUT OF *HER* EARS, TOO!
HI! I'M WENDY!

And look! Everyone here is just like me!
Our teacher is beautiful. We get to call her by her first name.
HELLO! I AM YOUR TEACHER, DORN!
Dor
And she looks like Snow White! Soon, I adore Dorn every bit as much as the seven dwarfs adored the real Show White. Dorn teaches us math...
5
...and reading...
Pig
...and writing. The basics!

But Dorn also tries to teach us how to lip-read. She says that lip-reading is watching people's mouths move when they talk, so we can understand them better.
SOUND FROM HEARING AID
+
VISUAL CLUES FROM LIPS
=
UNDERSTANDING
HELLOOO
But this gets tricky, because many words sound similar and people's lips look the same when they are saying them:
MOP, MOB, MOM, BOP, BOB, POP, OR POM?
VASE OR FACE?
SHERRY, CHERRY, OR JERRY?
SUE OR ZOO?
Dorn explains how we're going to figure out what people might be saying.
I SEE A BEAR. I SEE A PEAR. "BEAR" AND "PEAR" LOOK THE SAME COMING OUT OF A PERSON'S MOUTH, DON'T THEY? YOU CAN'T JUST WATCH A PERSON'S LIPS. YOU HAVE TO BE A DETECTIVE AND WATCH FOR OTHER CLUES, TOO.
bear
pear
I AM READY!
bear

VISUAL CLUES
What do you see while a person talks to you?
A PEAR.
A BEAR.
CONTEXT CLUES
Where are you while a person talks to you? What's going on around you during the conversation?
Fresh Prod
A PEAR.
A BEAR.
HELLO!
GESTURAL CLUES
What does a person do with her hands and body while she talks to you? What kinds of faces does she make?
A PEAR.
A BEAR.

HUH?
BUT...
sometimes what a person is *doing* doesn't match up with what it *looks like* they're *saying*. It's easy to make mistakes!
I SEE A PEAR!!!
MMM! I SEE A BEAR!!!
YUCK!
So Dorn encourages us to practice at home.
BEAR.
care
share
PEAR?
bear
care
share
I make many discoveries about lip-reading:
OOBA LUB JUKKA
WA
MURMA ARF BR
PP
LO MOOFA U
M
① MUST SEE PERSON'S FACE AT ALL TIMES!
HUH-AYE. HUH-OW. ARRR. YOOOO?
② EXAGGERATED MOUTH MOVEMENTS ARE CONFUSING!
But wait! There's more!

GRRR...
FOO BAH GAH BEE AHFAH!
③ SHOUTING IS **NOT** GOOD!
MUFFA UFFA WUFFA HOW BUH WUH MAH UFFA BUFFA.
④ MUSTACHES AND BEARDS ARE BAD NEWS! (SORRY, DAD.)
HEE HEE GOB HAH GOOBAH BUBBY UBBA LAH MA BOP!
⑤ HANDS IN FRONT OF MOUTH ARE ALSO BAD NEWS!
Leaf Journal
WUH ARR YOOO BEE LA SHOO MAH WA.
⑥ WHEN IT GETS DARK, GIVE UP!
And finally:
⑦ GROUP DISCUSSIONS ARE IMPOSSIB TO UNDERSTAN
But I can't really make signs like these—I can't even *read* yet! It's hard to explain all this to anybody—except at school.

George, Sabrina, Terry, Wendy, Fred, and Jamie: they understand. Because they are just like me.
GEORGE
TERRY
FRED
ME
SABRINA
WENDY
JAMIE

But everything is still so new, and so different, for all of us. Most of the time we are lost, drifting along on our own planets.
But we are together in the same universe, at least.

Suddenly, summer is here again. When I say good-bye to my friends at Fisher School, I do not realize that I will never again be surrounded by kids who are just like me.
JUNE
NETS
The next day, I'm back in the neighborhood with Emma.
ARE YOU READY FOR SUPPER?
SUPPER!? BUT IT'S STILL MORNING!
NO—NOT SUPPER—SUMMER! SUMMMMMM-MMMMMER!
SUPPER! HEE HEE!
SIGH.

four

Soon after I say good-bye to my friends at Fisher School, I say good-bye to Emma, too.
BYE, EMMA. BYE, SNOOPY.
My family is moving.
We're leaving our small row house in the big city...
HOUSE FOR SALE
Roanoke
...for a big old house in a small town.
WOW.

My siblings and I meet some of the kids in our new neighborhood.
MAH MOM ADE YAW UM EL-HO!
ATT MAN OR OOPER MAN?
WHAT'RE THOSE THINGS COMING OUT OF HER EARS?
SHHH!
HMPH. I HEARD WHAT THAT ONE SAID JUST FINE.
And I soon discover that these neighborhood kids are crazy about their radio!
YAY!
FM
AM
One of the kids tries to be nice and turns up the radio super loud for me.
THERE! HOW'S THAT?
!
Here's what I wish I could say:
THANKS, BUT I CAN HEAR THE RADIO WITH MY HEARING AID JUST FINE! I JUST CAN'T UNDERSTAND IT, BECAUSE I CAN'T SEE THE FACES OF THE PEOPLE WHO ARE SINGING AND TALKING!
Here's what I actually say:
UH...THANKS.

So, the neighborhood kids sing along with the songs...
DON'T GO BREAKIN' MAH HEART! I COULDN'T IF I TRIED! OOH, OOH...
...and they laugh along with whoever is talking...
NAW BOPPA MO
HA HA HA HEE HA HEE HA HO
...and it all sounds like a foreign language to me.
MEE NEEBO OP SHHH BIP UKKA MO GOBBA OP GA GLOP FOOM AW BUMM OH
HUH?
The person on the radio says something...the kids laugh some more. And this time, so do I. But what about?
HA HA HA HA SO FUNNY HA HA HO HEE HEE HO HO HA
HEH HEH HA AH...
I can't explain it, but it's not just the radio situation that is making me feel so lonely in this new place. It's a feeling that lasts all summer long.
HA HA HA
WOW
BATMAN

Summer ends. I find out that I will soon start first grade in a new school.
WILL I BE IN A CLASS LIKE DORN'S CLASS?
NO, SWEETIE. THEY DON'T HAVE A CLASS LIKE THAT IN YOUR NEW SCHOOL. BUT YOU'LL BE GOING TO SCHOOL WITH YOUR NEW NEIGHBORHOOD FRIENDS!
YOU'RE GETTING A BRAND-NEW, SUPER-POWERFUL, JUST-FOR-SCHOOL HEARING AID THAT WILL HELP YOU HEAR BETTER!
IS IT SMALLER THAN THIS ONE?
WELL, IT'S BIGGER, BUT YOU'LL HEAR SO MUCH MORE! AND YOU CAN WEAR THE LITTLE ONE AT HOME!
THE NEIGHBORHOOD KIDS? A BIGGER AID?
Mom walks me to school on the first day. We've been here once before, and I already know where my classroom is. But I'm still scared.
I wear my favorite striped shirt. And underneath that shirt...
HAVE A GREAT DAY!
...well hidden, I hope, is my brand-new, superpowerful, just-for-school hearing aid: The Phonic Ear.
BYE, MAMA.
the Phonic Ear is under here!
X-RAY VIEW this way...

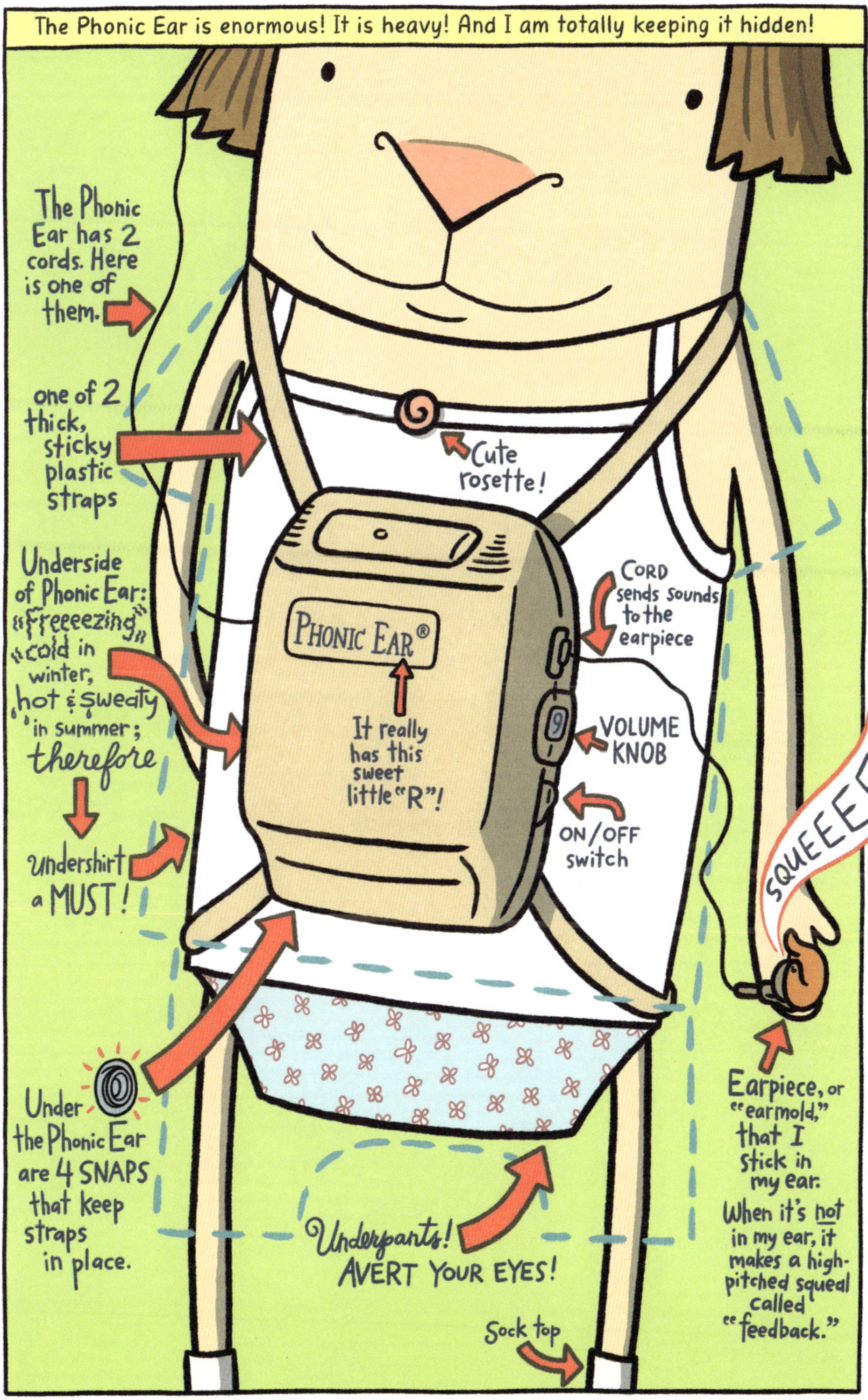

The Phonic Ear is enormous! It is heavy! And I am totally keeping it hidden!
The Phonic Ear has 2 cords. Here is one of them.
one of 2 thick, sticky plastic straps
Cute rosette!
Underside of Phonic Ear: "Freeeezing" cold in winter, hot & sweaty in summer; therefore undershirt a MUST!
PHONIC EAR®
It really has this sweet little "R"!
CORD sends sounds to the earpiece
VOLUME KNOB
ON/OFF switch
SQUEEEEE
Under the Phonic Ear are 4 SNAPS that keep straps in place.
Underpants! AVERT YOUR EYES!
Earpiece, or "earmold," that I stick in my ear. When it's not in my ear, it makes a high-pitched squeal called "feedback."
Sock top

The Phonic Ear is paired with a microphone that my teacher, Mrs. Lufton, is supposed to wear. When Mrs. Lufton speaks into the microphone, it sends signals to the Phonic Ear. These signals end up sounding like Mrs. Lufton is talking right in my ear!
welcome!
HELLO! WELCOME TO THE FIRST GRADE!
MICROPHONE
!
HELLO! WELCOME TO THE FIRST GRADE!
Mom was right! The Phonic Ear makes Mrs. Lufton's voice louder, just for me. It even clarifies her voice—really sharpens it! Even when I don't see Mrs. Lufton's face, I understand every word she says without having to lip-read at all.
CECE, IS THE MICROPHONE WORKING?
CECE, IS THE MICROPHONE WORKING?
YES!

The Phonic Ear is really powerful! I can hear Mrs. Lufton wherever she is in the entire classroom—and I can totally understand her, even if I can't see her.
DO YOU NEED TO GO TO THE BATHROOM?
DO YOU NEED TO GO TO THE BATHROOM?
I soon discover that I can hear Mrs. Lufton wherever she is in the *entire school building*.
HELLO, PRINCIPAL ECKHAR 'S SO NICE TO BE OUT OF MY CLASSROOM FOR A BIT!
I can hear her fussing at a classmate in the hallway right outside the classroom door!
JIMMY, THIS IS THE THIRD TIME THIS WEEK! *NO MORE TOYS!*
The microphone even picks up *other* people's voices! I can hear Mrs. Lufton and the other teachers all the way in the teachers' lounge!
THAT JIMMY MALONE IS MAKING MY LIFE ***HELL!***
MY, MY.
HE'LL BE YOURS NEXT YEAR, FRANCES.
SHE SAID H-E-DOUBLE HOCKEY STICKS!

Best—or worst—of all, I can even hear Mrs. Lufton when she USES THE BATHROOM!
squeeeeak
zzzzip
tinkle
tinkle
OH NO! HEE HEE!
AAAH...WHAT A RELIEF!
tinkle
tinkle
tinkle
TOILET PAPER?
WOPWOP
I KNOW WHAT'S COMING!
zzzzzzip!

FLUSH!
GEE! WHAT HAPPENED?
ER... NOTHIN'!
INCREDIBLE!
I HAVE AMAZING ABILITIES UNKNOWN TO ANYONE!
JUST LIKE BRUCE WAYNE USES ALL THAT CRAZY TECHNOLOGY TO TURN HIMSELF INTO BATMAN ON TV...

...I CAN USE MY OWN CRAZY TECHNOLOGY—THE *PHONIC EAR*—TO TURN *MYSELF* INTO A *SUPERHERO*, TOO! MY POWER? *SUPER HEARING!*

I WILL AMAZE EVERYONE—
HEY! WHAT ARE THOSE THINGS IN YOUR EARS? ARE YOU DEAF?
POP
ummm...

Superheroes might be awesome, but they are also *different*.
Batcave
And being different feels a lot like being alone.
BUBBLE OF LONELINESS
With the Phonic Ear, I have super hearing. Without it, I can't hear. *Am I deaf?*
MAYBE?

five

First grade is really lonely at first.
Wherever I am...
...it feels like I'm always inside my bubble.
CHIP
Is everyone staring at my hearing aid? At me?

But one day, the girl who sits next to me says:
HEY! WANT SOME FRITOS?
Fritos
Fritos
MY NAME IS LAURA, YOU KNOW, AND THAT'S A PRETTIER NAME THAN YOUR NAME. I THINK MRS. LUFTON IS *BEAUTIFUL*. YOU'RE A WEIRD KIND OF FUNNY. HEY! LET'S BE *BEST FRIENDS!*
UH...

It's all kind of sudden, so I think about it for a minute or two...
Frenz with Laura ?
YES
NO
Fritos
kinda pushee
duz not mine heerin aid
...and then I say:
OK?
POP!
Laura and I do become best friends...
THIS FEELS PRETTY GOOD!
...according to Laura, that is.
OK— HERE'S WHAT WE'RE GONNA DO...

Best Friends According to Laura is fun.
THAT'S SO NICE!
THANKS!
Sometimes.
MINE'S A BIT PRETTIER, THOUGH, DON'TCHA THINK?
UM... OK.
SHE'S CUTE!
THIS IS MISS BUNN!
MISS BUNN? HA, THAT'S A WEIRD NAME.
?
LET'S BUILD A SNOWMAN!
YEAH!
NO, NO! THE CARROT GOES HERE! IT'S A NOSE, SILLY!
!

Being best friends with Laura isn't perfect, but it sure beats being in the bubble. We stay best friends all through first grade, and we're still best friends during second grade. One day after school, Laura says:
YOU HAVE TO COME TO GIRL SCOUTS WITH ME TODAY. YOU'LL LOVE IT!
UM... OK?
TROOP 21
I join the Girl Scouts
Girl Scout Service Day
Camping at Dark Hollow

I meet new people in the Girl Scouts.
SILENTLY FLOWS THE RIVER INTO PEE, AND THE BARGES TOO GO POO POO POO!
HA HA!
BARGES, I WOULD LIKE TO POO WITH YOU, I WOULD LIKE TO POO POO POO POO POO!
HEE HEE! I WISH YOU WENT TO OUR SCHOOL!
HA HA! ME, TOO!
CAN YOU SPEND THE NIGHT NEXT SATURDAY?
But I'm not allowed to *keep* new people.
THAT'S *NOT* HOW YOU SING THE SONG. ANYWAY, CECE'S SPENDING SATURDAY NIGHT WITH ME. *RIGHT?*
UM, OK.

The following Saturday, at Laura's house...
BYE, MAMA!
WE'RE HAVING MAC AND CHEESE FOR SUPPER! AND WE'RE GONNA MAKE A CUSHION FORT!
HEY, LET'S PLAY THE DINING ROOM GAME WITH MY SISTER LUCY...
UM... WHAT'S THAT?
WELL, YOU AND LUCY JUST KINDA MARCH AROUND THE TABLE.
IS THAT IT?
IT'LL GET BETTER. HEE HEE! JUST KEEP ON MARCHING!

NOW, FLUFF—
NOW!
HEE HEE!
GET 'EM, FLUFF!!
EEK!
HA HA! YOU SHOULDA SEEN HOW FUNNY THAT LOOKED!
!
WHEW! THAT WAS FUN! NOW LET'S PLAY ANOTHER ROUND OF TWISTER! FLUFF, TOO!
WHAT!?
BUT YOU JUST LET YOUR DOG BITE ME!

I am glad to be back home after that sleepover!
DID YOU HAVE A GOOD TIME WITH LAURA?
WELL... NOT REALLY.
OH?
RING RING
IT'S LAURA. SHE WANTS TO PRETEND TO BE TWINS TOMORROW. SHE SAYS TO WEAR YOUR GREEN GIRL SCOUT T-SHIRT WITH YOUR RED SHORTS WITH THE WHITE STRIPES ON THE SIDE. OH, AND GREEN BARRETTES...
WAH WAH BOOLA BAH WA WAH
OH, SHOOT. THAT *DOES* SOUND FUN.
The next day...
Monday
IT WORKED! WE'RE TWINS!
Tuesday
SEE? WE'RE JUST LIKE SUSAN AND SHARON IN *THE PARENT TRAP*!
YEAH! WAIT—*WHO?*
Wednesday
OK. TOMORROW, WEAR YOUR BLUE SHIRT AND YOUR LEVI'S.
UM, SURE.
THIS IS SO MUCH *FUN!*
THIS IS STARTING TO GET *OLD...*
Thursday
OH! WHERE'S YOUR PALE BLUE SHIRT? YOU WERE ***SUPPOSED*** TO WEAR YOUR *PALE* BLUE SHIRT!
YOU JUST SAID ***BLUE!***

Friday
THIS COLOR GREEN LOOKS BETTER ON ME, Y'KNOW.
!
I KNOW LAURA LOOKS BETTER! AND IT'S NOT THE STUPID COLOR! SHE DOESN'T HAVE TO WEAR THIS STUPID HEARING AID ALL THE TIME! IT'S NOT FAIR!
I know I'll never be able to look just like Laura—or any other kid at school, for that matter.
YOU'RE SPENDING THE NIGHT TONIGHT, RIGHT?
UH...

Do I really want to spend any more nights with Laura?
Friends with Laura?
Yes
No
1. Gave me Fritos in furst grade
2. Does not care about hearing aid
3. Good times.
1. Vary pushy.
2. Bad times
3. More bad times (Fl
4. Twin stuff
It *is* nice that Laura really doesn't seem to notice or care about the hearing aid...
?
...but a familiar feeling has returned.
WELL?
1. Vary pushy.
2. Bad times
3. More bad times (Fluff
4. Twin stuff
5. I am Lonely
I THOUGHT BEING BEST FRIENDS WITH LAURA WOULD BE A GOOD THING...
...BUT NOW I'M JUST *SO TIRED* OF BEING *PUSHED AROUND!*
WHAT WOULD *BATMAN* DO?
IT'S TIME TO *PUSH BACK!*
IT *IS* TIME TO PUSH BACK!

An evil smile crosses our hero's face as she hypnotizes Laura, aka Super Bossypants, with the Phonic Ear's Vicious Feedback Squeal!
SQUeee
With the speed of light, our hero hurls the Earmolds of Virtue at Super Bossypants...
TAKE THAT!
...and ties her up with the Cords of Intuition!
BWAH-HAH!
LUCKILY, I HAVE A SPARE SET OF MOLDS AND CORDS WITH WHICH TO HEAR YOUR FEAR!
GULP!
UNLEASH THE HOUND OF HORROR!
?
A dazed Super Bossypants shudders in terror when she realizes her fate!

Luckily, the On/Off Switch of Awesomeness enables our hero to ignore Super Bossypants' pathetic pleas for help!
AH...SWEET, SWEET SILENCE...
CLIK
WAIT—WHAT?
(CLIK!)
I SAID, ARE YOU SPENDING THE NIGHT TONIGHT OR WHAT?
OH YEAH. YEAH, I GUESS SO.

six

The summer after second grade, I get new behind-the-ear hearing aids to use at home. No more little hearing aid in the pouch for me! I'm excited until...
THESE ARE GREAT, MR. RIDENHOUR! CAN I USE 'EM AT SCHOOL?
ER, NO. THESE AREN'T LOUD ENOUGH—OR CLEAR ENOUGH. YOU'LL UNDERSTAND YOUR TEACHER A LOT BETTER WITH THE PHONIC EAR.
RATS. I WAS HOPING TO BE DONE WITH THESE DUMB CORDS AT SCHOOL, TOO.
What I *don't* get that summer is a new friend. Here's what summer with Laura feels like:
HEY! LET'S: A) WALK TO THE 7-ELEVEN! B) GO SWIMMING! C) MAKE MILKSHAKES! D) SING THE DO-RE-MI SONG!
THOSE ALL SOUND FUN! I'LL BITE!
I AM THE WORM OF GOOD TIMES!
GOTCHA!
UH-OH!
OK, NOW WE CAN DO A, B, C, OR D—BUT *MY* WAY, *RIGHT?*
GLUB.
HOW DO I GET OUT OF THIS?

The night before the first day of third grade, I say a little prayer:
DEAR GOD, I AM READY FOR A NEW FRIEND THIS YEAR. PLEASE, COULD YOU WORK IT SO THAT LAURA AND I ARE IN DIFFERENT CLASSES? THANK YOU, AMEN.
My prayers are answered!
WHO'DJA GET?
MRS. IKLEBERRY.
OH NO! I GOT MRS. BLAIR!
WHEW!
WELL, WE'LL STILL GET TOGETHER AFTER SCHOOL, RIGHT?
UM...YEAH. SURE!
But maybe I should've been more careful with that prayer.
I'VE SPENT SO MUCH TIME WITH LAURA, I DON'T *KNOW* ANYONE ELSE! AND ARE THEY STARING AT MY *CORDS?*

A few weeks after school starts up, a new girl joins our class.
CLASS, THIS IS GINNY. SHE JUST MOVED HERE FROM GEORGIA. SAY HELLO, EVERYONE. GINNY, HAVE A SEAT THERE NEXT TO CECE.
...NEXT TO CECE.
UM...HI.
HI.
It feels like Ginny is always watching me.
In fact, she watches me for weeks...
HERE'S THE MICROPHONE, MRS. IKLEBERRY.
...until finally she asks:
IS. THAT. AAAY. HEAR-ING. AAAID?
OH...UM... I GUESS.
RATS!

One day after school, Laura comes over.
I'M GLAD I COULD COME OVER!
YEAH. IT'S BEEN A WHILE...
On our way upstairs, we hear some strange sounds coming from the kitchen.
HEE HEE ha ha hee ha Snort!
WHAT'S THAT?
HUH?
It's Mom! And some strange woman I've never seen before...
HEE!
HA!
MOM? SMOKING?
GIRLS, THIS IS MRS. WAKELEY! YOU MIGHT KNOW HER DAUGHTER GINNY, FROM SCHOOL?
Ginny? Oh, I know Ginny.
GIRLS, SHOW GINNY UPSTAIRS. MRS. WAKELEY AND I HAVE SOME MORE TALKING TO DO.
HEE HEE!

UM, GINNY, RIGHT? WELL, CECE AND I HAVE BEEN BEST FRIENDS EVER SINCE FIRST GRADE! AND I'M SPENDING THE NIGHT WITH CECE THIS COMING WEEKEND, RIGHT, CECE?
UM...YEAH, I GUESS SO, IF YOU WANT.
OH-KAAAY...
Up in my room, Ginny spots something:
HEY! IS. THAT. A. RICH-ARD. SCA-RRY. BOOK? I. LOVE. RIC-HARD. SCA-RRY!
ME, TOO!
WHY IS SHE TALKING TO ME LIKE THAT? SHE DOESN'T TALK TO LAURA THAT WAY!
RICHARD SCARRY!?!? I CAN'T BELIEVE YOU GUYS LIKE THOSE BOOKS. THOSE BOOKS ARE FOR BABIES. THEY'RE BABY BOOKS!
I WASN'T TALKING TO YOU, LAURA.
WOW! DID SHE JUST SAY THAT?
AN-Y-WAAY. I. HAVE. AAY. BU-SY-TOWN. PLAAY-SET. MAY-BE. YOU. CAN. COME. AND. PLAAY. WITH. IT.

A PLAYSET!? THAT'S EVEN MORE FOR BA—
UM—IS THAT YOUR MOM CALLING?
Laau-raaaa! Yoohoo
OH, SHOOT. THAT IS MY MOM. CECE, THIS FRIDAY, RIGHT?
UM...MAYBE? BYE!
THAT LAU-RAAA SURE BOSS-ES YOOO AH-ROUND. SHEEE'S LIKE THE SNOOOW QUEEEEN IN NAR-NI-A OR SOME-THING.
THE SNOW QUEEN? THAT'S HILARIOUS! AND I LIKE NARNIA, TOO!
ANY-WAAY...WHO IS THIS PRE-CIOUS BUN-NY?
UM...THAT'S MISS BUNN.
GINNY SURE IS NICE! BUT HOW CAN I TELL HER THAT IT'S HARDER TO UNDERSTAND HER WHEN SHE TALKS SO LOUD AND SLOOOOOOW?
WHAAT AAY CUTE NAME!

My mother and Mrs. Wakeley are fast becoming best friends. This means that Ginny and I are spending a lot of time together, too. We discuss important matters...
WAN-NA SEE MEEE MAKE AAARM-PIT FAARTS?
...we play with our stuffed animals...
KISSY, KISSY!
...and we laugh over just about anything.
HA HA! NOW IT SAYS, "GEE, YOUR HAIR *SMELLS!*" HEE HEE!
Ginny even joins my Girl Scout troop.
ALICE THE CAMEL HAS FORTY HUMPS!
YOU *ARE* SPENDING THE NIGHT TONIGHT, *RIGHT?*
UM, GINNY ALREADY ASKED ME TO. SORRY.

I really, really like Ginny. She's funny. She's weird. We love all the same things. So what's the problem? It's the way she talks to me—and the way she talks *about* me.
CEE-CEE. DOO YOO WANT MYYY PEEA-NUT BUTT-ER SAND-WICH?
UM, NO THANKS.
ARGH! I REALLY NEED TO TELL GINNY TO STOP TALKING TO ME LIKE THAT!
CHIPS
CEE-CEE, THIS IS *KREEE*-STEN!
BUT WHAT IF I *DO* TELL HER AND I HURT HER FEELINGS? I DON'T WANT TO MAKE HER MAD AT ME!
CEE-CEE IS MY DEAF FRIEND. SHE IS ACT-U-A-LLY ONE OF MY BEST-EST FRIENDS!
GULP! GOOD GRIEF! I *HAVE* TO TELL HER. TOMORROW. MAYBE.

I said I would tell her tomorrow. Well, it's tomorrow. What am I gonna do?
HEY! LET'S LIS-TEN TO MY BRO-THER'S MON-TEEE PY-THON RE-CORD!
OH NO.
HA HA HA! I'LL EX-PLAIN IT IN A SEC!
HEH HEH HEH.
LET MEEE STOP THE RE-CORD NOW...THEY ARE SING-ING AAY SONG THAT GOES, "I'M A LUM-BER-JACK AND I'M OOH-KAY...
... I SLEEEP ALL NIGHT AAND I WORK AAALL DAAAY!" HAR!
THIS IS TOTALLY DRIVING ME NUTS!
HI-LAR-I-OUS, RIGHT?
HEH, YEAH.
AND NOW FOR THE NEXT BIT!
OH? UM...YAY?
RATS.

I'm so frustrated with Ginny!
SNORT!
She can hear and understand everything so easily.
I LOVE THIS PART!
HA HA!
Heck, everyone in the whole world can probably hear and understand this stuff.
Monty Python is so very funny
HA HA HA HA
HA HO HO
HA HA HA HA HA HEE HA
What should I do? What would *Batman* do? All the data says that Ginny is *so close* to being a perfect friend. But obviously, there *is* a problem:
GOOD:
SO FUNNY
WEIRD IN A GOOD WAY
LIKES THE THINGS I LIKE
NOT SO GOOD:
MAKES A *HUGE* DEAL ABOUT MY HEARING!
AAAAHHH!!!

Our hero trembles with frustration! She grabs the offending record...
I. JUST. CAN'T. TAKE IT ANYMORE.
WAIT!
...and throws it against the wall...
OH!
...shattering it—forever!
HA!
LISTEN UP!
OH NO!
THIS SECONDHAND MONTY PYTHON STUFF IS DRIVING ME CRAZY! AND WHAT'S MORE—
—YOU DON'T HAVE TO TALK TO ME SO LOUD AND SO SLOW! I CAN'T STAND IT!

WHY'DJA SAY THAT? I WAS JUST TRYING TO HELP YOU!
OH NO! DID I ACTUALLY SAY THAT LAST PART OUT LOUD? AT LEAST I DIDN'T REALLY BREAK THE RECORD!
UM...I'LL JUST PUT THIS AWAY... FOREVER...SNIFF!
GINNY?
Oh, what have I done?
UM...ARE YOU OK?
I DUN-NO. MAY-BE YOU'D BETT-ER GO. ON. HOME.

seven

School. Friends. No friends. The Phonic Ear. It's all so exhausting. I need a break.
So I watch TV.
I watch anything that's on. Everything, in fact. Soap operas. Cartoons. Old sitcoms. New sitcoms. Dramas. Even commercials! And the crazy thing is...
...I love TV...
...even though it's so hard to understand what the people on it are saying!
HUH?

TV isn't like the weird foreign movies that Dad takes me to every once in a while.
ENGLISH SUBTITLES!!
oh, I'm not so sure about this
OOOH! WORDS! I LOVE THEM!
GRANDIN
MOUR
URM...I'M NOT SURE THESE MOVIES ARE ALL THAT APPROPRIATE FOR YOU... THAT WAS A LOT OF SKIN...
BUT, DAD, I LOVE HAVING THE WORDS! I ACTUALLY KNOW WHAT'S GOING ON!
Sadly, TV does *not* have subtitles.
HUH?
UGGA MAWHAW OOP GAH MUMMA MUH GOO AH OH MEEMO...
I *try* to lip-read the people on TV...
C'MON! JUST ONE WORD?
BAB! MUMMA MAW! GOOBA BOO AH
...but it's really, *really* hard to do!
WHAT IN HECK IS GOING ON?

I keep watching, though. Some shows are fairly easy to lip-read, like soap operas:
Actor's face takes up the whole screen: easy to see lips!
I
Actor speaks slowly and dramatically...
AM
IN
LOVE
...and it's pretty much a guarantee that LOVE will come up!
WITH WANDA!

But who wants to watch *soap operas?* They're so mushy...
BUT...I *NEED* YOU, JIM!
AND I WANT TO HAVE...
...A *BABY* WITH YOU!
UM, SORRY. I LOVE *WANDA!*
...and so boring!
IT'S THIRTY MINUTES LATER...
...AND WE'RE STILL HAVING THE SAME CONVERSATION!
I OBVIOUSLY NEED TO FIND SOMETHING BETTER TO WATCH!

Aha! Cartoons! I love cartoons! But lip-reading cartoons? Impossible!
BLAH WAH FRED LOO MA WAH HA HOOH WALAWA...
Cartoon lips are not like real lips at all. Not even close.
OOGA MOO BLAH HAH GOO BOO HAW!
Unreadable!
But I love cartoons anyway. The characters do so many funny things that I can see.
And hey, check it out! Here's a cartoon that doesn't have any talking at all!
Cat doesn't talk!
Mouse doesn't talk, either!
But as much as I love cartoons, even they can be pretty boring sometimes.
IT'S SAFE TO SAY THAT THE CAT REALLY, REALLY WANTS TO CATCH THE MOUSE. AGAIN.

I watch other shows on TV, too, even if they are not as easy to understand as soap operas and cartoons. I might catch a few of the words in these shows, but not many.
I see the person's face while she's talking. She looks worried. But she's talking so fast, and her lips are so small on the TV screen, that I can't understand her. Is John-Boy lost—or something worse?
MA! WE OOK EBBER WAR AN WE ANT FINE JOHN-BOY!
Uh-oh! Now I can see a different person's face. She is listening to someone who is talking—and that person is OFFSCREEN! Will John-Boy be OK?
UGGA SHUFFA GOO BLAH BLAH HA OOKIN WAMAH WAH!
Now I can mostly just see the speaker's REAR END!
AGGA BOOP BAH WAHAH BICK! CHUBBA UBB OH GOBBA!
WHO KNOWS WHAT'S GOING ON NOW? I SURE CAN'T LIP-READ A BUTT!
Now NOBODY on the TV is talking. But I think I hear something that sounds like talking! It's the... dreaded VOICE-OVER!
AN GOO HON BOY GABBA WAH GAH WHA BEE GOO BA BA MAMA.
I STILL HAVE NO IDEA WHAT HAPPENED TO JOHN-BOY!

If I'm watching TV with somebody who doesn't know me well, like a neighborhood kid whose mom is visiting my mom, then that kid almost always asks:
YOU'RE THE KID WHO CAN'T HEAR, RIGHT? WHY NOT JUST TURN UP THE VOLUME?
OH BROTHER. HOW CAN I EXPLAIN THIS?
Well, here's what happens when I turn up the TV:
WAH BESS MAH WAWA GAH ANDY! YOO GOOLA FA BERRY GAH BOOLA!
Before
WAH BESS MAH WAWA GAH ANDY! YOO GOOLA FA BERRY GAH BOOLA!
Same scene, with volume UP!
UM, IT DOESN'T MATTER HOW LOUD IT IS. IT'S JUST HARD TO UNDERSTAND, I GUESS.
SO WHY ARE YOU WATCHING IT, THEN?
UM...

Well, I guess I watch TV because the folks on it are there for me whenever I want them—and they don't care if I can hear them or not!
OINK!
Not so there for me are my older siblings—Ashley and Sarah. They are often busy doing mysterious older-kid things:
WANNA PLAY OLD MAID?
HUH? UH...NOT REALLY.
DO YOU WANNA PLAY OLD MAID?
UH...NO!
AND DON'T YOU DARE TELL MOM!
But when they aren't busy, they watch TV. A lot of TV. If I want to spend any time with Ashley and Sarah, it's gotta be while watching TV. So that's what I do.

However, the shows that Ashley and Sarah watch are impossible to understand.
emotionless MUMBLER!!
MURK PROOP TIBBA MAWHAW...
Lip-reading + surgical masks= IMPOSSIBLE!!
SHMAR MUMBAMUMBA GUMBA...
But luckily they are nice enough to tell me what the people on TV are saying...
WHAT'S GOING ON?
WE'LL TELL YA... LET'S WAIT FOR A COMMERCIAL...
...without ever being obnoxious about it.
SO, TRAPPER JOHN IS TELLING HAWKEYE THAT FRANK HAS MADE A BIG MISTAKE...
...AND HOT LIPS KNOWS ALL ABOUT IT!

Every now and then, ABC shows an hour-long movie made especially for kids.
abc AFTER SCHOOL SPECIAL
Sometimes these movies are super corny. We *really* love the ones that are.
HAR! THIS ONE'S GONNA BE *GOOD!*
When this one starts—*wait a minute!* Is she wearing what I *think* she's wearing?
I CAN'T BELIEVE IT! SOMEONE LIKE *ME*— ON THE *TV!*
YOO AH AH EFFO! MUMMBA GUH!
WHAT JUST HAPPENED? WHAT DID SHE *SAY?*

WELL—UM...
WELL, WHAT?
...AHEM...
UM...THE ONE KID CALLED THE OTHER KID—AHEM— "DEAFO."
WHAT? DEAFO? REALLY? THAT'S JUST MEAN!
UH... HEE HEE...
What is wrong with me? Why in the world am I laughing? It's really not funny at all!
HEE HEE HA HEE HAHA!

I GOTTA GO PEE...
HIC! HEE HEE...
WHEW!
DEAFO, HUH?
HEH HEH...WELL, IF
THAT KID IS "DEAFO"...
...AM I
"DEAFO"
TOO?

HEY, DEAFO.
DEAFO.
YOU WANNA CALL ME "DEAFO"? GO AHEAD!
YEAH, THAT'S RIGHT!
JUST CALL ME...
EL DEAFO.

eight

A few weeks after my argument with Ginny, I see her handing out little cards. I wonder what they say. Will I get one, too?
UH—SORRY A-BOUT EAR-LI-ER. HERE.
SHE'S STILL TALKING FUNNY? OH WELL.
You're invited!
What.
When. Friday
Where. Ginny's
A BIRTHDAY PARTY AND A SLEEPOVER? WOWEE!
UH...
A SLEEPOVER, HUH?

WELL, I DON'T LIKE GINNY ANYWAY!
AND MY NEW BEST FRIEND, BETH, IS SPENDING THE NIGHT WITH ME THAT NIGHT, SO HA.
I know I should feel bad about this...
UMM...
...but I don't.
...WELL, BE SURE TO PLAY THAT DINING ROOM GAME WITH BETH! SHE'LL LOVE IT!
Things may not be perfect with Ginny, but yeah, I'll go to her party!
I CAN'T WAIT!
When. Friday Apr. 16
Where
A WHOLE WEEK? RATS.

After a long week of waiting, the day of the sleepover is finally here! I pack as soon as I get home from school.
OH BOY!
Packing List:
toothpaste (possibly just for show)
toothbrush
cute pj's
clean shirt for tomorrow
sleeping bag
extra hearing aid batteries (I do NOT want to run down and miss everything!!!)
Pill-pill
clean underwear
socks
Miss Bunn (may need to keep hidden??)
birthday present for Ginny!
...UM, I GOTTA GO...YES, YES—LISTEN, CECE IS *BREATHING* ON ME—OK—BYE!
OK ALREADY! WE'RE GOING!

Mom drops me off at Ginny's house...
HAVE FUN! AND JUST ASK MRS. WAKELEY TO CALL ME IF YOU NEED ANYTHING.
I'LL BE FINE, MOM!
BYE!
HI!
SO, WHO ALL'S HERE?
YOU'RE THE FIRST, AC-TU-A-LLY. BUT IT'LL BE CAR-RIE, ELL-EN, AND MISS-Y. I CAN'T *BE-LIEVE* MISS-Y'S COM-ING—SHE IS *SO POP-U-LAR!*

The other guests arrive...
CARRIE
1. Shy, but nice.
2. Draws really good horses.
3. Soft voice. So hard to hear!
UH, HI? I BROUGHT SOME CANDY. WANT SOME?
HUH?
ELLEN
1. Asks too many personal questions.
2. Always smells good.
3. Not shy at all!
WHERE ARE THOSE CORDS THAT ARE USUALLY COMING OUT OF YOUR EARS?
WHY DO YOU WEAR OVERALLS SO MUCH?
ARE YOU DEATH?
And then there is...
MISSY
OH! IT'S THE LITTLE DEAF GIRL FROM MRS. IKLEBERRY'S CLASS! GINNY'S TOLD ME ALL ABOUT YOU!
1. Help.

CECE IS MY DEAF FRIEND.
YES, I KNOW. SHE'S ADORABLE!
DOES SHE KNOW SIGN LANGUAGE? I CAN TEACH HER SOME RIGHT NOW!
OK, HERE'S HOW YOU MAKE AN "A"...
NEAT!
GRRR... I KNOW THAT!
...AND HERE'S A "B"!
THIS IS SO FUN!
UM...
CEEE...
UM...I GOTTA GO, UH, FIND SOMETHING...

In spite of that rough beginning, I start having a great time at Ginny's sleepover. We celebrate Ginny's birthday...
...and explore her older brother's bedroom...
KEEP OUT
...and play lots of Twister.
RIGHT HAND BLOOOOO, CEE-CEE!
GOOD GRIEF!

But then things start to go downhill again.
HEY! THE TV GUIDE SAYS THAT SOMEWHERE IN TIME IS COMING ON IN TEN MINUTES! IT'S MY FAVORITE!
OH NO. DID SHE SAY SOMEWHERE IN TIME?
SQUEEEEE!
OH! I LOVE THAT MOVIE!
UH-OH.
YAY!
EEK!
OH, SO DREAMY!
Oogah blah mumba
ICK.
OH, YOU POOR THING! CAN YOU EVEN HEAR THE TV?
UH, I CAN HEAR IT. I JUST CAN'T UNDERST—
WE'LL JUST TURN UP THE VOLUME!
I CAN HEAR IT! I JUST CAN'T UNDERSTAND IT! AND I'M NOT A "POOR THING"!

One hundred and three minutes later...
I LOVE THIS MUSIC. I HOPE IT'S WHAT THEY PLAY AT MY FUNERAL...
YAWN!
WHAT A FABULOUS MOVIE!
YEAH...SO, WHAT'S NEXT?
UMMM...
HEY! LET'S DO A MAKEOVER—
ON CEE-CEE!
CEE-CEE, WE THINK YOU ARE CUTE! BUT YOU COULD BE CUTER! WE WANT TO DO YOUR HAIR AND MAKEUP!
WHAT A GREAT IDEA!

No, no, *no*. I absolutely *hate* makeup and all that girly stuff.
NOT GONNA DO IT! I DON'T WANT TO!
HERE'S THE SIGN FOR "YES," AS IN, OH, *YES* YOU *ARE*!
COME *ON*, CEE-CEE! DON'T RUIN THE FUN!
BUT I DON'T *WANT* A MAKEOVER! *REALLY*!
Y'ALL, WAIT! CAN PEOPLE WHO WEAR HEARING AIDS ALSO WEAR MAKEUP?
HUH?

THAT'S THE DUMBEST QUESTION I EVER—WAIT A MINUTE! HERE'S MY CHANCE TO GET OUT OF THIS!
UM...
...I DON'T BELIEVE WE CAN. MESSES UP THE HEARING AIDS, AND STUFF.
I THOUGHT SO!
BUMMER.
WHEW!
OK, SINCE THAT DID-N'T WORK, HOW A-BOUT WE GO A-HEAD AND GET IN OUR SLEEP-ING BAGS?
I GUESS.

Thankfully, after all that awfulness, the party starts to get fun again.
...AND YOU SHOULDA SEEN MARY KISSING THAT BOY FROM MS. HUFFMAN'S CLASS! ALL THIS *MWAH MWAH MWAH!*
HEE HEE!
THIS COULD GET *INTERESTING!*
SQUEAL!
But then—
CLIK!
—Ginny turns the lights out!
HA HA HEE HEE SQUEE HEE HA HA HO HA HEE HEE!
OH NO!
I CAN TELL THEY'RE LAUGHING, BUT WHAT ABOUT? I NEED TO *SEE!* DID GINNY DO THIS ON PURPOSE? IS SHE *MAD* AT *ME?*
WELL, *RATS!* IF I ASK GINNY TO TURN THE LIGHTS BACK ON, SHE'LL BE EVEN MADDER AT ME. *EVERYONE* WILL BE MAD AT ME!

HA HA HEE CEE HA HA CEE HA MUMMBA HA HEE CEE HA HA GOBBA WOBBA HA HO HO HEE HA HA!
I HATE THIS! ARE THEY TALKING ABOUT ME? ARE THEY LAUGHING AT ME?
I CAN'T TAKE IT ANYMORE!
I gather up my stuff in the dark, and I feel my way out of the basement...
...and up the stairs.
MRS. WAKELEY? WILL YOU CALL MY MOM? I DON'T FEEL SO GOOD...

I am relieved that Mom doesn't ask any questions on the way home.
UM...HI, DAD. CAN I WATCH TV WITH YOU AND MOM?
Oh, I'm so glad to be home. What a night. I wish I'd told those girls what I think!

Our hero, the mighty El Deafo, is tied up by a band of pajama-wearing Super Villains!
The Super Villains interrogate El Deafo—and torture her with more Somewhere in Time! But El Deafo is strong...
WHAT ARE THOSE CORDS FOR?
WHY DO YOU WEAR OVERALLS SO MUCH?
ARE YOU DEATH?
wah wah wah
YES, I'M DEATH! AND YOU ARE NEXT ON MY LIST!
HERE'S A TASTE OF YOUR OWN ROPE—AND SOME OF THAT FUNERAL MUSIC YOU WANTED, TOO!

But it's not over yet for El Deafo! She is accosted by another menacing foe...
EEK!
I AM SUPERMISSY! PREPARE FOR BEAUTY, MY LITTLE DEAF FRIEND!
Our hero is more than ready!
READ MY LIPS! NOBODY TOUCHES THIS FACE!
HOW ABOUT A MAKEOVER, MISSY? WHAT PLEASURE THIS GIVES ME, YOU'LL NEVER KNOW!
TA-DA!
EEK! I'M HIDEOUS!

At long last, El Deafo faces the mightiest foe of all, the dastardly SuperGinny.
DON'T EVER CALL ME YOUR DEAF FRIEND AGAIN. OR YOUR FRIEND. DID YOU TURN THOSE LIGHTS OFF ON PURPOSE?
I DUNNO.
UH...I'M SORRY!
SORRY ISN'T GOOD ENOUGH. GOOD-BYE.
ZZZZZZZZZZZ...

nine

Ah, summer. Three months of freedom. Three months of bliss. Three months of *not* wearing the Phonic Ear.
But summer ends—as it always does—with the beginning of a new year of school.
YAWN
UGH. TIME TO WEAR THIS AGAIN!
SIGH...
FOURTH GRADE! I CAN'T BELIEVE IT! ARE YOU EXCITED?
UM, MAYBE A LITTLE...
Actually, except for the Phonic Ear, I am *very* excited. A new year!
BUS

Just like in previous years, our mornings start in the gym. I see Ginny, but I avoid her. I want to sit with kids who don't know me. Maybe I can pass myself off as a hearing person.
But I'm not very good at doing this.
HI, I'M BONNIE. WHAT'S YOUR NAME?
UH— CECE.
WELL, HEY. I'VE TOLD EVERYONE ELSE, SO I MIGHT AS WELL TELL YOU: MY GRANDMA MAKES PIE.
UH...COOL!
WHAT!?
UH...
?
I *SAID*, MY GRANDMA MAY DIE!
OH! *OH!* I AM SO, SO SORRY!

THAT'S OK. SAY! WAIT A MINUTE—
I CAN'T BELIEVE I DID THAT! ARGH!
—ARE YOU DEAF? IS THAT WHAT THE CORDS ARE FOR?
OH NO!
BECAUSE I...
KNOW...
SIGN LANGUAGE!
HELP.
What's wrong with sign language? Nothing. But some of the people doing sign language? At me? Some people put on a real show when they start signing—almost like mimes!
CE—
—CE...
IS ANYONE WATCHING THIS?

...and some people end up saying phony-baloney stuff when they sign...
...YOU...
...ARE SPECIAL!
PLEASE. STOP.
...and sure enough, when somebody signs at you like that, everybody else stares at you!
Argh! I wish I could turn into El Deafo in these situations.
I DO NOT KNOW THESE MYSTERIOUS HAND SIGNALS, STRANGER! BUT I DO HAVE A GREAT POWER! I CAN READ YOUR LIPS!
GULP!
If only it were that simple.
SOME LIP-READER I AM. "MAKES PIE"? GOOD GRIEF.
SNIFF!

Back at home, after a long first day of school...
WELL, HI! HOW WAS SCHOOL?
IT WAS OK. BUT SOME GIRL STARTED SIGNING AT ME!
OH, CECE. I KNOW YOU DON'T LIKE IT WHEN PEOPLE DO THAT. SHE WAS PROBABLY JUST EXCITED TO MEET SOMEONE LIKE YOU, AND TO SHARE WHAT SHE KNOWS WITH YOU...
SOMEONE LIKE ME?
MAYBE YOU SHOULD LEARN SIGN LANGUAGE! IT WOULD GIVE YOU A NEW WAY TO TALK TO PEOPLE. IT COULD BE FUN!
MOM! I DON'T WANT TO!
I HEARD THERE'S A SIGN LANGUAGE CLASS THAT JUST STARTED UP AT CHURCH!
OH NO!
MAMA, PLEASE DON'T MAKE ME DO THAT!
LET ME LOOK INTO IT FIRST, SWEETIE. IT MIGHT REALLY BE USEFUL TO YOU.
MOM! NO!

One evening a few weeks later, Mom takes me to a classroom at our church.
LOVE
We meet our sign language teacher, Mrs. Blankenship, who, I admit, is very nice.
HELLO!
AND WELCOME—
TO SIGN LANGUAGE!
FIRST, IS ANYONE HERE DEAF OR HARD OF HEARING?
UM—MY DAUGHTER IS...
MOM!

WELL, THAT'S LOVELY. FIRST, LET'S TALK ABOUT AMERICAN SIGN LANGUAGE. IT'S THE MAIN LANGUAGE USED BY DEAF PEOPLE—AND IT IS *VITAL* FOR THEIR COMMUNICATION WITH OTHER DEAF PEOPLE AND WITH THEIR FAMILIES AND FRIENDS.
MANY HEARING FOLKS THINK THAT SIGN LANGUAGE IS A SIMPLE LANGUAGE—BUT THAT IS NOT TRUE AT ALL!
BLAH, BLAH, BLAH—*UH-OH!*
SIGN LANGUAGE IS QUITE DIFFERENT FROM SPOKEN ENGLISH.
IT'S A VERY RICH LANGUAGE—A VERY *COMPLEX* LANGUAGE.
MY HEARING-AID BATTERIES ARE RUNNING DOWN!
WHY DON'T I EVER REMEMBER TO BRING EXTRA BATTERIES?
SO, WE'LL BE LEARNING THE BASICS
WHEW. LIP-READING IS *HARD* WITHOUT SOUND.

LET'S START WITH THE ALPHABET. HERE'S "A".
HEY, I KNOW *THAT!* THAT'S "A"! I GUESS SHE'S TEACHING THE ALPHABET. *HMPH.*
?
Thirty long—and silent—minutes later, the class finally ends. I lip-read my mother saying, "What did you think?" I say, "How do *I* know? My hearing-aid batteries ran down."
And then Mom says, "*See?* Maybe sign language could be useful to you after all!"
ME saying "I don't think so!"

Every Thursday night, I find myself back in that dumb old classroom...
HERE IS "THANK YOU..."
WEEK 2 MANNERS
CE-CE, THANK YOU FOR BE-ING MY FRIEND!
UM... YEAH.
HERE'S A FUN ONE: GIRAFFE!
WEEK 3 ANIMALS
THESE ANIMAL SIGNS ARE SO CUTE! TRY ONE!
HMPH.
"elephant"
OK! LET'S PARTNER UP AND ASK EACH OTHER HOW SHE FEELS...
WEEK 4 FEELINGS
HOW AM I FEELING? TAKE A WILD GUESS.
"How are you feeling?"

I can't believe that my own mother can't see that I am absolutely miserable.
JUST TRY IT—"FATHER"!
WEEK 5
FAMILY
PLEASE?
COME ON, CECE! YOU CAN DO IT! FATHER!
IT'S REAL EASY, SEE? FATHER!
ARGH!
GOODNESS, CECE! EVERYONE'S JUST HOPING THAT YOU'LL PARTICIPATE MORE. NEXT WEEK, PLEASE JOIN US. YOU'LL SEE HOW FUN IT IS, OK?
HOW WILL I EVER GET OUT OF THIS?

So what, I haven't been "participating." Mom totally makes up for it—she *loves* to sign!
MOM, CAN I HAVE THE LAST BANANA?
"yes"
CAN I PLEASE USE DAD'S X-ACTO KNIFE?
"no"
MOM, CAN I—
"wait"
"toilet?"
MOM! NO!
OH! IT'S ALMOST TIME FOR OUR CLASS!
"time"
NO. MORE. CLASSES!!!
MUMBA OH ABLA OOG UMMA BAH...

Our hero, the mighty El Deafo, has met a most worthy opponent: her own mother! How can El Deafo free herself from the shackles of this weekly humiliation?
DO YOU NEED TO TINKLE BEFORE I LOCK THESE HANDCUFFS...FOR GOOD?
PLEASE, MIGHTYMOM! STOP SIGNING AT ME!
Our hero unleashes her Powers of Persuasion...
OH MIGHTYMOM, CAN YOU NOT SEE THAT I AM ABLE TO TALK TO YOU RIGHT NOW WITHOUT USING MY HANDS?
YOU'RE SO CUTE WHEN YOU BEG!
pat pat
HOW DOES SHE DO THAT?
THIS VICIOUS FEEDBACK SQUEAL WILL HYPNOTIZE YOU AND YOU'LL FORGET ALL ABOUT THAT DUMB CLASS!
THAT SOUND DOESN'T BOTHER ME. AT ALL.
SQUeeeeee
RATS. MIGHTYMOM IS AMAZING.

Enraged, El Deafo busts out of the handcuffs...
...and unfurls her torpedo-like wrath onto her own mother!
KAPOW
OW!
OK, OK, YOU'VE MADE YOUR POINT. WE'RE GOING HOME.
DID I REALLY DO THAT?
JESUS IS LOVE

WHAT IN THE WORLD WAS THAT ALL ABOUT?
OH, MOM— I'M SORRY...
...BUT I HATE THAT CLASS! EVERYBODY SIGNING AT ME! LIKE I ALREADY KNOW SIGN LANGUAGE, JUST BECAUSE I'M DEAF!
NO ONE'S SIGNING AT YOU— THEY'RE TRYING TO SIGN WITH YOU—TO HELP YOU!
WELL, I HATE IT!
AND AS FAR AS "HELPING"— IT'LL HELP PEOPLE STARE AT ME, IS WHAT IT'LL DO! "LOOK AT THAT DEAF GIRL! ISN'T SHE SPECIAL!"
WELL—YOU ARE SPECIAL—
MOM!
—JUST LIKE EVERY KID IS SPECIAL.
OH, GOOD GRIEF.
MOM THINKS "SPECIAL" MEANS "GREAT," OR "COOL." IF ONLY! "SPECIAL" MEANS "YOU'RE NOT LIKE ME! YOU'RE WEIRD!" I HATE THAT WORD!

LISTEN. WE DON'T HAVE TO CONTINUE THE CLASS. JUST DON'T BE SO HARD ON THE PEOPLE WHO TRY TO HELP YOU. SOMEDAY YOU MIGHT ACTUALLY *WANT* THEIR HELP.
WHEW!
We stop for a treat on the way home...
SHAKES
SUNDAES
PIES
HAMB
CHEES
FRENC
...and then—believe it or not—we see a couple arguing...
...in sign language!
THAT IS AMAZING.

I COULD HAVE LEARNED HOW TO DO THAT IF I HAD "PARTICIPATED." AND MAYBE I SHOULD HAVE...
...BUT THEN OTHER PEOPLE WOULD STARE AT *ME* THE WAY I'M STARING AT THAT COUPLE. *RIGHT?*
OH, WHY DO I EVEN *CARE* WHAT OTHER PEOPLE THINK?

ten

As I ride the bus home from school one day, I realize just how many kids live on my street. We practically fill up the whole bus! But not one of them is in my grade.
MATT, 5th grade
MARTHA, 3rd grade
DAVID, 3rd grade
JOE, 3rd grade
CATHERINE, 1st grade
JOHNNIE, 3rd grade
HELEN, 5th grade
JIMMY, 3rd grade
Jill wuz here
DAN, 2nd grade
FROM A DIFFERENT NEIGHBORHOOD
ME, 4th grade
TRISH, 1st grade
SUZIE, 5th grade
FROM A DIFFERENT NEIGHBORHOOD
BLAKE, 3rd grade
There had been a girl in my class, and we watched *The Monkees* at her house after school sometimes. But she moved away.
Jill wuz here
The other kids on the street *are* nice, though, especially the older ones. They often include me in their games and stuff...
HEY, WE'RE PLAYING KICKBALL WHEN WE GET HOME. WANNA PLAY?
But *I* think they've been *told* to be nice to the deaf kid. And anyway, I always seem to ruin those games of theirs!
KAH MON!
OH DA BAW!
?
GA WOO! OH ETT!
UH, THANKS. BUT I HAVE A LOT OF HOMEWORK...
OH. OK.

Kickball? *Ha!* I'm gonna do what I usually do after school: watch TV.
CECE, IT'S GINNY. SHE WANTS TO KNOW IF YOU'D LIKE TO COME OVER.
UH—NO THANKS. TELL HER I'M BUSY.
GINNY?—UH—CECE IS KIND OF BUSY TODAY—UH—TELL YOUR MOM HI FOR ME, OK?—BYE...
YOU HAVEN'T SEEN GINNY IN AGES! WHAT'S GOING ON? DID YOU HAVE A FIGHT?
KINDA.
WANT TO TALK ABOUT IT?
NOT REALLY.
WELL, I'M SORRY ABOUT THAT. BUT I DON'T APPRECIATE LYING TO YOUR FRIEND. SO I SUGGEST YOU HURRY UP AND GET "*BUSY.*"
I'm relieved that I don't have to get together with Ginny. I guess I *could* play some kickball with the kids down the street. Or not. I don't know *what* to do.
SIGH...

Somehow, being alone is always easier for me. But it's still, well, *lonely*!
OH, WOE...
WHAT I *NEED* IS A SIDEKICK!
!
THERE'S THAT THIRD-GRADER, MARTHA. I WONDER WHY *SHE'S* NOT PLAYING WITH THE OTHERS? SHE USUALLY DOES...
HEY!
POP
UMM OBA HEE UN TAY ALOO!
UM—HOLD ON A MINUTE!
I *THINK* SHE WANTS ME TO COME OVER...

MOM! THE KID ACROSS THE STREET— *MARTHA*? I THINK SHE WANTS ME TO COME OVER! CAN I?
I *KNEW* GOING OUTSIDE WOULD DO YOU GOOD! BUT LET ME WATCH YOU CROSS THE STREET.
FLO
GEE! DOES YOUR MOM REALLY HAVE TO WATCH YOU CROSS THE STREET? AREN'T YOU IN FOURTH GRADE? I'M IN THIRD, AND MY MOM DOESN'T DO THAT!
THAT'S JUST MY MOM FOR YA, I GUESS.
HUH. WELL, ANYWAY, FANCY MEETING YOU HERE! D'YA LIKE THAT? MY MOM SAYS IT ALL THE TIME. "FANCY MEETING YOU HERE!" I'M MAKING DIRT SOUP. WANNA HELP?
UH...
SURE!

THIS HERE DIRT SOUP MAKES ME THINK OF *LITTLE HOUSE ON THE PRAIRIE*. DO YOU WATCH THAT SHOW?
I *LOVE* THAT SHOW!
HEY! LET'S PRETEND THAT ***WE'RE*** *LITTLE HOUSE ON THE PRAIRIE!* DO YOU WANNA BE MARY OR LAURA?
CAN I BE LAURA?
YEAH! I'LL BE MARY. ***WHOA!*** THAT SCARLET FEVER DID A ***NUMBER*** ON ME! JOHN-BOY, THAT YOU?
HA HA HA! JOHN-BOY—HEE HEE! MARTHA, I MEAN *MARY*—YOU'RE IN THE ***WRONG SHOW!***
WHAT IF MARY ENDED UP ON *STAR TREK* OR SOMETHING?
BEAM ME BACK TO THE PRAIRIE, SCOTTY!
hee hee ha ha
ha hee hee
ha ha hee ha
hee
YOU KNOW, IT'S FRIDAY AND ALL—YOU SHOULD ASK YOUR MOM IF YOU CAN SPEND THE NIGHT!
I WAS THINKING THE ***EXACT SAME THING!***

Yay! Mom said yes to the sleepover! I start packing—and I start thinking, too.
MARTHA IS SO FUNNY! I'M ACTUALLY GLAD SHE'S NOT IN MY GRADE, BECAUSE IF SHE WAS, SHE'D SEE MY GIANT HEARING-AID AND THOSE CORDS COMING OUT OF MY EARS. SHE'D *KNOW* I WAS DEAF. BUT SHE *DOESN'T* KNOW, BECAUSE SHE HASN'T NOTICED MY BEHIND-THE-EAR AIDS. WELL, I *THINK* SHE HASN'T NOTICED. I MEAN, SHE DOESN'T SHOUT AT ME, OR MOVE HER MOUTH ALL FUNNY, OR TRY TO SIGN AT ME. SHE'S NOT BOSSY, EITHER! NO *WAY* AM I GONNA LET HER FIND OUT. IT MIGHT RUIN *EVERYTHING!* OH, WE'RE GONNA HAVE SO MUCH FUN TONIGHT!
YAY!
WE ARE GONNA HAVE SO MUCH FUN TONIGHT!
I WAS JUST THINKING THE *EXACT SAME THING!*

Inside Martha's house...
MOM, THIS IS CECE!
FANCY MEETING YOU HERE!
THAT'S MY DAD...
REALLY?
DREAMY!
AND HERE ARE MY LOONY SISTERS! PROTECT ME!
MOM!
DAD'S PICKING UP LONG JOHN SILVER'S AND WE'RE EATING IN FRONT OF THE TV!
A TV SUPPER? REALLY!?
YEAH! WHAT WOULD YOU LIKE DAD TO ORDER FOR YOU? A MUMBLE ABBO OR AH ISH UPPA?
HUH? I BETTER PRETEND THAT I KNOW WHAT SHE SAID!
UH...
...I'LL HAVE WHAT YOU'RE HAVING?
OK! TWO FISH SUPPERS COMING RIGHT UP!
FISH? ICK. WELL, AT LEAST MARTHA DOESN'T SUSPECT ANYTHING DIFFERENT ABOUT ME...

We have a great time! We eat...
I BETTER LAUGH SO SHE'LL THINK I UNDERSTAND!
...we play...
HEY, YOU WITH THE FACE! HOW MUCH FOR THESE TEENY PEAS? AND BY THE WAY, THERE'S A TINY SPILL IN TINY AISLE THREE!
THOSE ARE MINE! *MINE!*
TOYS
...and we run all over the house, yelling and laughing.
AWOOOOOOOOOOOOOO!
MARTHA ANN!

AHEM! GIRLS, IT IS WAY PAST YOUR BEDTIME...
AWWW...
WELL, WE CAN STAY UP AND TALK!
CAN WE LEAVE A LIGHT ON?
SURE THING!
LOOK DOWN YOUR SHIRT AND SPELL "ATTIC"!
A-T-T-I-C? MARTHA ANN!
...YOU KNOW WHAT WE SHOULD DO TOMORROW? WE SHOULD WALK DOWNTOWN AND GET CANDY BARS AND DRINKS AND STUFF...AND THEN WE CAN MAKE MORE DIRT SOUP...
...SO SLEEPY...
...AND SO I SAID, WHAT IS THAT
STINKIN' SMELL? AND
THAT'LL BE
SAID THAT!
EYED LOOK
OFF! I FELT
I GOTTA GET SOME SLEEP! SURELY SHE WON'T NOTICE IF I TURN OFF MY AIDS...
CLIK!

AH, SWEET SILENCE...
ZZZZZZZ...
tap tap
UH-OH...
I lip-read Martha saying, "Did you just turn your hearing-aids off on me?"
OH NO! I'VE RUINED EVERYTHING!
UMMM... I'M SO SORRY!
CLIK!
WAIT! MARTHA KNOWS ABOUT MY HEARING-AIDS?

OH, THAT'S OK. IT'S HILARIOUS HOW YOU CAN DO THAT! I WISH I COULD DO THE SAME THING WITH MY SISTER!
errkkzzz Shork zzz
I REALLY AM SORRY. BUT HOW DID YOU KNOW THAT I CAN'T HEAR VERY GOOD?
OH, THE NEIGHBORHOOD KIDS TOLD ME.
SO YOU'VE KNOWN ALL ALONG?
SURE!
HUH!

WELL, *HEE HEE*—I'LL LET YOU SLEEP NOW. BUT PINKIE SWEAR THAT WE CAN DO THIS ALL THE TIME?
OH— *YES!*
UH, EXCUSE ME—
POP
UH, I'M HERE ABOUT THE AD. *SIDEKICK WANTED?*
AH—YES. SO, WHAT ARE YOUR SUPERPOWERS?
WELL, I HAVE *TOTAL RECALL* OF MOST TELEVISION SHOWS...
I AM LOYAL, BRAVE, AND TRUE...

AND I CAN MAKE YOU LAUGH UNTIL YOU PEE IN YOUR PANTS!
WELL, THAT DOES IT! YOU'RE HIRED!
BY THE POWER OF THE PINKIE, DO YOU SWEAR TO JOIN THE FIGHT AGAINST BOREDOM AND LONELINESS, AND TO NEVER SWERVE FROM THE PATH OF TRUE FRIENDSHIP?
YES, I DO!
And thus, Martha Claytor, by the hand of fate, is transformed into that most glorious superhero of all, the True Friend.

eleven

Fourth grade ends, and it's summer! Summertime with Martha is awesome.
WE CAN GET LIMEADES AT THE DRUGSTORE!
OW! UM, YEAH!
Walking downtown in bare feet!
AAAH...
Cooling feet on drugstore floor!
It can't get much better than this!
CHECK OUT MY BEE-HIND!
OOH, FUNKY!
Roller-skating on the sidewalks!
Or can it?
LOOKS LIKE A NEW FAMILY IS MOVING INTO THE CARTERS' OLD HOUSE!
ACE Movers
LET'S CHECK IT OUT!
YEAH!

We cross the street. Some other kids have come out to meet the new neighbors, too.
HOLY COW! THEY ARE SO GOOD-LOOKING!
HI!
The new kids look like rock stars! Like the Partridge Family or something!
Or maybe even *movie stars*! Good *grief*, the beauty!
HI! WE'RE THE MILLERS!
Kathy
Caryn
Steve
Mike

I'M MIKE. WHAT'S YOUR NAME?
UH...UH...
THIS IS CECE! SHE LIVES TWO DOORS UP! I'M MARTHA, AND I—
—UH...WE GOTTA GO! COME ON, MARTHA!
HUH?
HEY! I WAS STILL TALKING! WHAT'S THE MATTER? WAIT! OH MY GOSH—YOU LIKE HIM?
WHAT!? NO! NO WAY!
CECE AND THE NEW KID SITTIN' IN A TREE, K-I-S-S-I-N—
MARTHA, STOP!
I DON'T EVEN KNOW THE KID! SO DON'T YOU DARE TELL ANYBODY ANYTHING! 'SPECIALLY NOT MY MOM! 'CAUSE YOU'RE WRONG!
OOH! A WIDDLE BOYFRIEND!

Martha *is* sorta right. But I'm not going to tell her—or anyone else—that I like this *Mike Miller* very much.
Instead, I decide to spy on him. I want to learn *everything* about him—but *secretly*!
FBI
SHHHH!
TOP SECRET FiLes
DO NOT OPEN
This means You!
I watch Mike Miller very carefully. Day...
EY! ETT ETT UMM ANNY AHH DAH EEEN AHKAH!
UH-HUH...
...after day...
UM...AH OOH OH ENN AAH ERRAH HAH UMBAY EY AAY?
UH-HUH...
...after day!
ETT ER URN A MIR AH OOP!
UH-HUH...
UH...I GOTTA GO. I WANNA WRITE SOMETHING DOWN...
UH-HUH.

Top Secret Facts about Mike Miller
1. He is cute.
2. He is good at dribbling a basketball.
3. I am pretty sure he is nice.
4. I think we could be friends!????
5. I think I might li'
I GOT BORED WHEN YOU LEFT. WHAT'RE YOU WRITING?
NOTHIN'!
WELL, WHILE YOU WERE—AHEM—"WRITING," I WENT AND TALKED TO MIKE MILLER! YOU SHOULD TALK TO HIM—HE'S NICE! ANYWAY, IT TURNS OUT THAT HE HAS A TRAMPOLINE IN HIS BACKYARD...AND HE SAID WE CAN USE IT!
YOU TALKED TO MIKE MILLER!? A TRAMPOLINE? THAT WE CAN USE? I KNEW HE WAS NICE!

This could be it! A real opportunity to talk to *Mike Miller*!
WELL, LET'S GO RIGHT NOW AND ASK HIM IF WE CAN USE THE TRAMPOLINE!
UH... OKAY!
GO ON— KNOCK!
KNOCK KNOCK
HELLO?
UH...
CAN WE JUMP ON THE TRAMPOLINE?
UH...JUMP...
SURE!
LET'S *GO*! HE SAID YES!
...JUMP...

ARE YOU SURE YOU DON'T LIKE HIM? 'CAUSE I THINK YOU DO!
RATS! WE SHOULDA ASKED HIM TO JUMP WITH US!
OH, I'M SURE!
TOTALLY SURE.

A magnificent jump off the trampoline—and El Deafo is suddenly soaring through the air!
She spies a boy—but not just any boy.
It's Mike Miller, aka SUPERCRUSH!!!
PERHAPS THE ALL-POWERFUL ROSETTE ON MY UNDERSHIRT WILL LURE MY SUPERCRUSH INTO MY LOVING ARMS!
WOW!
MEGA-MAGNIFICATION of the ALL-POWERFUL ROSETTE! Behold its astounding beauty!

UM, HI, CECE. HOW ARE—
AHA!
WHA!?
SNAGGED ON THE THORN OF THE ALL-POWERFUL ROSETTE!
COME CLOSER!
YES, MY LADY...

HEY!
UH, YOUR FRIEND—MARTHA?—
SHE WANTED ME TO TELL YOU
THAT SHE WENT ON HOME.
HEH HEH...
UH...BYE!
I *KNEW* HE WOULD BE NICE!

twelve

It is a very bouncy summer. Sometimes I jump on the trampoline by myself...
...but most of the time, I jump with Martha.
WE SHOULD ASK MIKE TO JUMP WITH US SOMETIME!
NOW, WHY WOULD WE DO THAT?
BECAUSE YOU LIKE HIM?
NOT THAT MUCH! HEE HEE!
I quickly change the subject...
WHEW! LET'S DO SOMETHING ELSE!
HOW ABOUT TAG? BETCHA CAN'T CATCH ME!
YOU'RE ON!

HEE HEE!
HEY! NO FAIR! I'M STILL STUCK ON THE TRAMP!
WHOOP!
I'VE ALMOST GOT HER NOW!
OW!

OW, OW, OW!
OH NO! WHAT HAPPENED? ARE YOU OK?
I THINK SO— I RAN RIGHT INTO THAT TREE!
DOES IT LOOK BAD? AM I BLEEDING?
UH...I THINK WE'D BETTER SHOW YOUR MOM...

MAMA?
OH DEAR. IT LOOKS BAD.
UH...UH...
BUT NOT *TOO* BAD! NOTHING THE DOCTOR CAN'T FIX! I'LL GET A WASHCLOTH...
DON'T WORRY, IT'S ALREADY FEELING SO MUCH BETTER!
UH, I GOTTA GO...

I come back from the doctor's office with eye medicine and a fancy eye patch.
CAN I GO SHOW MARTHA MY NEW EYE PATCH? SHE'LL LOVE IT!
GREAT IDEA!
HEE HEE! SHE'LL LAUGH WHEN SHE SEES THIS!
KNOCK KNOCK
Martha answers the door.
AHOY THERE, MATEY! I LOOK LIKE A PIRATE, DON'TCHA THINK?
UH... UH...

DID SHE JUST THROW UP? IT DOESN'T LOOK THAT BAD, DOES IT?
And then—Martha disappears!
MARTHA? ANYBODY?
I wait a bit, and then Martha's mom comes.
I'M SO SORRY ABOUT YOUR EYE! LISTEN, MARTHA ISN'T REALLY UP TO TALKING JUST YET. SHE KIND OF THINKS THAT ALL OF THIS IS HER FAULT!
OH, BUT IT ISN'T HER FAULT! NOT AT ALL! IT WAS AN ACCIDENT!!
I CAME OVER TO SHOW HER THAT I'M FINE! HONEST!
I KNOW, HONEY, I KNOW. DON'T WORRY. SHE'LL COME AROUND.
SNIFF!

The next day, I write Martha a note. I put a koala bear sticker on it, too. She'll like that!
Dear Martha,
How are you? I am fine, and so is my eye. It was NOT your fault!!!!
At all!!!
I miss you.
Love, Cece
I run across the street to give her the note. I don't even wait for Mom to watch me.
MARTHA— WAIT!
HI, CECE. UM...MARTHA IS STILL UPSET. BUT SHE'LL COME AROUND. IS THAT NOTE FOR HER?
PLEASE WILL YOU GIVE IT TO HER?
OF COURSE, DEAR.
The next day...
HEARD ANYTHING FROM MARTHA?
NO. WILL YOU TRY CALLING HER FOR ME?
...UM, YES, PATSY, I SEE. WELL, TELL HER THAT CECE REALLY, REALLY MISSES HER AND THAT SHE DOESN'T BLAME MARTHA ONE BIT... OK, SURE. BYE.
I'M SO SORRY...
SHE'LL NEVER "COME AROUND."

I try to give Martha some time, but one week later, I'm back at her door.
MY EYE'S ALL BETTER! SURELY WHEN SHE SEES THAT, SHE'LL BE MY FRIEND AGAIN!
KNOCK KNOCK
MARTHA? LOOK! I'M ALL BETTER! NO MORE EYE PATCH!
UH, I GOTTA GO. I THINK MY MOM'S CALLING ME...
MARTHA, *COME BACK HERE!* ARE YOU GONNA BE LIKE THIS FOR THE REST OF THE SUMMER?
OR *FOREVER?*
I'M QUITTING THE SIDEKICK BUSINESS...

QUITTING!? YOU CAN'T DO THAT! YOU PINKIE SWORE! WHAT ABOUT THE PINKIE SWEAR??
I UNDID MY PINKIE SWEAR WHEN I HURT YOUR EYE, EL DEAFO! AND I JUST CAN'T DEAL WITH THE GUILT!
BUT YOU DIDN'T HURT MY EYE! AND IT'S ALL BETTER! IT'S NOBODY'S FAULT!
THEN I'M NOBODY. GOOD-BYE, EL DEAFO!
OH NO!

WHAT AM I GONNA DO WITHOUT HER?

thirteen

Weeks pass. In late August I get a letter that says who my fifth-grade teacher's gonna be.
SINKLEMANN? HUH. GEE WHIZ, SUMMER IS GONNA BE OVER SOON...
...AND STILL NOT EVEN A PEEP FROM MARTHA.
RING
BUT WAIT! COULD IT BE?
RING
WELL, YES! SHE'D LOVE THAT. YES—YES, IT HAS BEEN A LONG TIME...
FINALLY!
IT'S GINNY! SHE WANTS TO COME OVER. YOU'RE NOT "BUSY" RIGHT NOW, SO I WENT AHEAD AND SAID YES.
GINNY?
IT WILL BE SO NICE TO SEE YOU PLAYING AGAIN WITH—
GINNY?!
YES, GINNY. SHE'S BEEN CALLING ALL SUMMER! I THINK SHE WANTS TO MAKE UP WITH YOU, SO I SUGGEST YOU AT LEAST BE NICE TO HER, OK?
GOOD GRIEF. THANKS A LOT, MOM. REAL HELPFUL.
OK.

One hour later...
HI, CEE-CEE!
SHE'S THE SAME AS EVER. EXCEPT... WHEN DID SHE —AHEM— GROW SO MUCH?
I HAV-EN'T SEEN YOU IN FOR-EV-ER! UM...ARE YOU STILL MAD AT ME?
NAH. NOT REALLY.
URG. I HAVE NO IDEA WHAT TO DO WITH HER!!
HEY, I KNOW! WANNA JUMP ON A TRAMPOLINE? THE NEW KID ON THE STREET HAS ONE, AND HE'S REAL NICE ABOUT LETTING US USE IT!
MIKE MILLER...
OK!
At Mike Miller's house...
YEAH, YOU CAN USE THE TRAMP. HEY, UM, WHO'S GONNA BE YOUR TEACHER NEXT YEAR? I GOT SINKLEMANN.
SINKLEMANN?
ME, TOO!

I MEAN—AHEM—ME, TOO.
UH...COOL. WELL, BYE.
AHM ENN MEH SINN-A-MANN HASS OOO!
SIGH...THAT MIKE MILLER IS ADORABLE!
AHM ENN MEH SINN-A-MANN HASS OOO!
AND HE'S GONNA BE IN MY CLASS! MY CLASS!
A-HEM! I SAID, I'LL BE IN MIS-SUS SINK-LE-MANN'S CLASS, TOO!
HUH? OH, SORRY! I MEAN, THAT'S GREAT!
REAL-LY? I WAS-N'T SURE YOU'D EVEN CARE!
OH, I DO!
MIKE MILLER...
REALLY!

A week later, I wake up on the first day of school, and I am excited!
WONDERFUL WORK, CECE!
A NEW TEACHER!
COOL NEW SCHOOL SUPPLIES!
CECE, CAN YOU HELP ME WITH MY MATH?
YOU PLUS ME EQUALS US, BABY!
CUTE NEW BOYFRIEND?
BUT WAIT A MINUTE! I ONLY WEAR THIS GIANT THING AT SCHOOL—
—WHICH MEANS THAT MIKE MILLER HAS NEVER SEEN THE PHONIC EAR BEFORE! NO WAY IS HE EVER GONNA LIKE ME NOW!
YOU LOOK WEIRD! I'LL ASK SOME OTHER GIRL ABOUT THE MATH...
WHAT!?

The first day back at school is always difficult: I have to walk past everyone's desk to give my new teacher the microphone.
If there's one thing I hate, it's showing the microphone to a teacher for the first time...
...mostly because everyone *stares* at me as I go up to the teacher's desk.
And today, *Mike Miller* is staring at me, too!
I WISH HE COULDN'T SEE MY CORDS! HE MUST THINK I'M A TOTAL *WEIRDO!*
MRS. SINKLEMANN, THIS IS THE MICROPHONE. AND HERE'S WHAT YOU DO...
Mrs. Sinklemann

Actually, it's totally worth giving Mrs. Sinklemann the microphone each day. Otherwise, I would miss out on all the fun. She's an awesome teacher...
I'VE GOT A GIRL NAMED BONEY MALONEY...
SHE'S AS SKINNY AS A PIECE OF MACARONI!
...and her classroom is *the* place to be.
I'M SO THRILLED TO SHARE MY BUTTERFLIES WITH ALL OF YOU!
But one day during storytime, I realize that Mrs. Sinklemann is looking kinda fuzzy.
...HIS FLESH IS ROTTING OFF THOSE MEAN BONES, AND MAGGOTS ARE CREEPING IN HIS EYE SOCKETS AND CRAWLING OUT HIS NOSE HOLES...
And the kids look kinda fuzzy, too. Could it be love that's making my eyes all blurry?
"THAT'S A LIE, THAT'S A DISGUSTING LIE," TURTLE SHOUTED.

The blurriness gets worse. And now I have a serious problem!
abolish
challenge
courteous
jubilation
We're taking a vocabulary test today, and I can't read the words that we're supposed to define!
ARE THOSE EVEN WORDS?!
I want to ask Mrs. Sinklemann for help, but where is she?
Oh!—I can hear her! And it sounds like she's talking to another teacher:
BAD DAY, MRS. WEST?
OH, THOSE BRATS! THEY'RE GONNA SEND ME TO AN EARLY GRAVE!
HMMM. THAT MEANS SHE'S NOT EVEN IN THE ROOM! I BET SHE'S IN THE TEACHERS' LOUNGE!
HEY, GINNY!
WHAT'S THE FIRST WORD ON THE BOARD? I CAN'T SEE IT! EVERYTHING'S SO BLURRY!
SHHHH!

MISS BELL! JUST WHAT DO YOU THINK YOU'RE DOING? THIS IS A TEST! COME UP TO MY DESK THIS INSTANT!
WHERE DID SHE COME FROM? I THOUGHT I WAS SAFE!
Everyone's staring at me—again!—and for once I wish it was hearing-aid related!
CECE, I'M GOING TO HAVE TO GIVE YOU A ZERO...
A WHAT?! BUT I STUDIED SO HARD FOR THAT!
DID YOU, DEAR?
I DID!—SNIFF— HONEST!
I'M NOT GONNA CRY...
I CAN'T CRY! NOT WITH EVERYONE LOOKING AT ME!
HIC!
STOP CRYING! STOP!

WAH!
THERE, THERE. GO GET A DRINK OF WATER, AND TRY TO SETTLE DOWN.
DID MIKE MILLER ACTUALLY SEE ME CRYING? I BET HE THINKS I'M A BIG BABY!
WHY DIDN'T MRS. SINKLEMANN GIVE ME A CHANCE TO EXPLAIN?
AND NOW SHE'S TREATING ME LIKE A CHEATER! AND OH NO! MOM AND DAD! WHAT WILL I TELL THEM? AND WILL THEY BELIEVE ME?
I return to my classroom, but before I open the door, I listen.
IT SOUNDS LIKE MRS. SINKLEMANN IS DOING MATH NOW. I GUESS IT'S SAFE TO GO BACK IN...
I HOPE NO ONE'S LOOKING AT ME! I CAN'T EVEN SEE IF ANYONE'S LOOKING AT ME!

Somehow, I make it back to my desk. It's a long, long day after that.
OH NO! IS IT TIME TO GO HOME ALREADY?

I get home before Mom does. And when she arrives, I am ready...
UH...MOM?
OH, HI!
UM, I SAW MRS. SINKLEMANN JUST TEN MINUTES AGO AT THE GREEN MARKET. SHE TOLD ME WHAT HAPPENED. I KNEW YOU'D BE UPSET, SO I BOUGHT YOU SOMETHING...
HERE YA GO.
Hostess FRUIT PIE REAL FRUIT FILLING
OH, MAMA! A HOSTESS PIE! AND *CHERRY*, EVEN!
WANT TO TELL ME WHAT HAPPENED?

I COULDN'T SEE THE BOARD AND I ASKED GINNY FOR HELP AND MRS. SINKLEMANN THOUGHT I WAS CHEATING AND I GOT A ZERO! *THAT'S* WHAT HAPPENED! *HONEST!*
SOUNDS TO ME LIKE YOU BETTER GET YOUR EYES CHECKED. YOU MIGHT NEED GLASSES!
YOU MEAN, YOU *BELIEVE* ME?
OF *COURSE* I DO, CECE. NOW, LET ME PUT THE GROCERIES AWAY...
GLASSES? HMM.
BUT, *OH!* THIS IS *SO GOOD!*
THANKS, MAMA!

fourteen

Sure enough, Mom is right. On Saturday, I get glasses—and they are *incredible*.
I CAN SEE!
I CAN ***SEE!***
The faraway stuff that had been so blurry? It's all so much clearer now!
HOLY COW! LOOK AT THOSE *LEAVES!*
BEFORE
AFTER
?
SLAW DOG
HOT DOG
CHEESEBURGER
HAMBURGER
FRENCH FRIES
ONION RINGS
AH! ONION RINGS!
BEFORE
AFTER
We eat out that day, and at the restaurant I discover that my glasses make everyone's *mouths* clearer, too—even faraway mouths. I can lip-read like never before.
OH MY GOODNESS! SHE JUST SAID SHE'S LEAVING HIM... *AND SHE* SAID *FUDGE*, BUT FOR *REAL!* THESE GLASSES ARE *AWESOME!*

After lunch, I experiment with my glasses. Off and on, off and on, over and over.
BLURRY...
CLEAR...
BLURRY...
CLEAR—HEY! IT'S *MARTHA!*
MAYBE I CAN IMPRESS HER WITH MY NEW GLASSES!
SHE'LL *LOVE* 'EM!
ZOWIE! THESE *SPELLBINDING SPECTACLES* CAN SPOT MY SIDEKICK FROM MORE THAN A MILE AWAY! AND JUST WAIT TILL SHE YIELDS TO THEIR *HYPNOTIC CHARMS!*

HELLO, SIDEKICK!
OH! I GOTTA GO— WHOA!
REPEAT AFTER ME: YOU WILL BE MY SIDEKICK AND MY TRUE FRIEND AGAIN...
I WILL BE YOUR SIDEKICK AND YOUR TRUE FRIEND AGAIN...
AND NOW YOU WILL PINKIE SWEAR IT...
AND NOW I WILL PINKIE SWEAR IT...
I KNEW THIS WOULD WORK!
SHE KNEW THIS WOULD WORK...
MARTHA! HI!
I KNOW THIS WILL WORK!
But I can see, all too clearly, that Martha still wants nothing to do with me.
RATS.

On Monday morning, I go to the bus stop wearing my brand-new glasses.
HEY! YOU GOT GLASSES!
C'MON, MARTHA, CHECK 'EM OUT! I'M KINDA LIKE HELEN KELLER "LITE" NOW, HEH HEH!
BLEH!
EW!
MARTHA, *WAIT!* THE GLASSES HAVE NOTHING TO DO WITH WHAT HAPPENED TO MY EYE! *HONEST!*

THAT'S THE SECOND TIME I'VE MADE MARTHA THROW UP! I DON'T THINK I'LL EVER GET HER BACK! HOWEVER...
...I AM SEEING MIKE MILLER BETTER! AND HE'S EVEN CUTER IN FOCUS!
UM...I THINK YOUR GLASSES MAKE YOU LOOK LIKE JOHN LENNON...
UH...UH...
HE EVEN KNOWS ABOUT THE BEATLES! SIGH...

fifteen

I love my glasses. Being able to see makes everything easier—especially at school.
OH! *NOW* I GET IT!
90° right angle
So I decide to really, *really* study.
AH! KNOWLEDGE IS POWER!
Maybe if I make good grades, here's what will happen:
DO YOU KNOW CECE?
YOU MEAN THAT *DEAF KID?*
NO! I MEAN THE *SMARTEST* KID IN THE *WHOLE SCHOOL!*
My hard work pays off in all my classes...
CECELIA BELL GRADE 5 SINKLEMANN
ENGLISH A
MUSIC S
MATH A
ART S
SOC. STUDIES A
SCIENCE A
PHYS. ED.
L. Sinklemann
Parent Signature

...except one: Physical Education, also known as P.E.
NOT SATISFACTORY?! WHAT?!!
CECELIA BELL GRADE 5 SINKLEMANN
ENGLISH A
MATH A
SOC. STUDIES A
SCIENCE A
MUSIC S
ART S
PHYS. ED. NS
L. Sinklemann
Parent Signature
Well, I know I'm not very athletic...
OOF!
OW!
NO WAY CAN I HIT THAT!
...and it's so hard to know what to do when everybody's yelling different things at me.
MEEMEEE!
BLAH WAH!
TOE DABAW AH EEBA!
OOGA!

The P.E. teacher, Mr. Potts, doesn't help my situation at all. In fact, I live in fear of him!
AWRIGHT, KIDS! LET'S BREAK IT UP INTO TWO TEAMS FOR SOME MAJOR KICKBALL ACTION!
UH...DON'T FORGET THE MICROPHONE, MR. POTTS...
And he really does treat us as if we are two separate teams: the athletic kids...
Y'ALL ARE AWESOME!
...and everyone else.
HAR! GOOD LUCK!

Luckily, we don't have P.E. every day. But today we do—and we're playing *kickball*.
I GUESS I'LL TAKE CECE...
AT LEAST I GOT CALLED BEFORE HENRY FOR ONCE!
Kickball is a disaster. Whether I'm kicking...
MISSED—AGAIN!
...or trying to throw the ball—I *know* I stink.
AH WOO BAH! OH ETT EEAH!
OBB GOBBA BAW!
BAW
FIBBA
I sneak in a little break during the game, and suddenly, I hear Mr. Potts talking to himself.
DANG MICROPHONE'S ALL TANGLED UP IN MY WHISTLE! I'LL JUST—OOPS!
PHYS ED
OH NO!

I watch as the microphone falls toward the Hardest Surface in the Known Universe—the gym floor!
HERE IT COMES!
KA-BOOM
OW!!!

WHOOPSIE! HEH HEH...
WHOOPSIE?! IS THAT ALL YOU'VE GOT?
It's broken! Mr. Potts broke my microphone!
CRACKLEZZZZZZZZCRINKLECRA
ZZZZ CRAKKKKK ZZZZZZZZZ
HELLO? HELLO?
TESTING, 1-2-3...
HELLO?
I don't understand anything now. Mrs. Sinklemann seems so far away...
SO WHEN WE OOGA MOO, WE MUMBLE BLAH GAH!
?
bear
bare
read read
red reed
NEVER,
...and she never stays still. Even with my glasses, I can barely see enough to lip-read.
I SAW MOOLEE OOMA! MOOLEE OOMA HEY, HEY...
?
Thank goodness Mrs. Sinklemann is sympathetic.
I WROTE DOWN YOUR HOMEWORK... IT'LL BE BETTER TOMORROW, I BET!
SNIFF!
I'm still kinda worried, though.
GRADE 5
SINKLEMANN
ENGLISH F
MATH F
MUSIC NS
ART NS
PHYS. ED. NS
Parent Signature
WHAT'S GONNA HAPPEN?

When I get home, I put on my behind-the-ear aids, and I show Mom the broken microphone. She calls my audiologist.
...UH-HUH, I SEE. SILVER SPRING, *MARYLAND?* OK, LET ME GET A PENCIL...
WE'RE SENDING THE MICROPHONE AND YOUR HEARING AID TO MARYLAND. I GUESS YOU'LL HAVE TO WEAR YOUR BEHIND-THE-EAR AIDS TO SCHOOL FOR A WHILE.
FOR HOW LONG?
UM...EVERYTHING WILL COME BACK TO US IN THE MAIL IN FOUR TO SIX WEEKS.
FOUR TO SIX *WEEKS!?*
I WON'T BE ABLE TO UNDERSTAND *ANYTHING!* I'LL FAIL *EVERYTHING!*
WHAT AM I GONNA *DO?*
FOUR TO SIX *WEEKS* WITHOUT MY *SUPERPOWERS?* I DON'T KNOW WHAT *I'M* GONNA DO, EITHER—BUT IT AIN'T GONNA BE PRETTY!

The next morning, for the first time ever, I actually miss putting on the Phonic Ear.
I FEEL SO... SO NAKED!
I GUESS I SHOULD BE HAPPY TO HAVE THESE AIDS. BUT HOW AM I GONNA UNDERSTAND MRS. SINKLEMANN? I'M NOT THAT GOOD AT LIP-READING!
At school...
BLAH BLAH WAH MUMWAH HOO. AN ATTS EE ENN!
ARGH! I CAN'T FOLLOW THE BOOK IF SHE'S COVERING HER FACE WITH IT! AND I THINK I JUST MISSED THE ENDING! OH, FOUR TO SIX WEEKS? OF THIS?
Later that day...
MRS. SINKLEMANN TOLD ME TO TELL YOOO THAT WE'VE GOT PEE-EE NEXT.
YEAH. I KNOW.
AND I AM READY.
WITH OR WITHOUT SUPERPOWERS, I AM STILL EL DEAFO— AND I AM OUTRAGED!

Today in P.E., we are supposed to do tests for the Presidential Physical Fitness Award.
HE SAYS THE GIRLS HAVE TO DO "FLEXED-ARM HANGS" LIKE BECK-Y IS DO-ING!
YIKES.
A flexed-arm hang means you have to stay in a pull-up position and keep your chin over the bar for as long as you can stand it!
00:10
00:02
00:23
Now it's my turn.
ALRIGHT, BELL. LET'S SEE WHAT YOU CAN DO, HEH.
LOOK OUT, POTTS! PREPARE TO BE AMAZED!

Our hero is suddenly fueled by rage!
THAT MAN HAS COST ME MY SUPERPOWERS...
00:20
...MY GOOD GRADES...
00:40
...BUT NOT MY GOOD NAME!
00:64
SIXTY-FOUR SECONDS! I AM EL DEAFO! I AM A CHAMPION!
It's a world record! The president of the United States of America himself arrives to present El Deafo with her hard-earned award!
MOVE OVER, POTTS!
OUR GREAT NATION PRESENTS THIS PHYSICAL FITNESS AWARD TO YOU, EL DEAFO, FOR YOUR REMARKABLE FEATS OF SKILL AND TALENT!
PRESIDENTIAL PHYSICAL FITNESS AWARD

SIXTY-FOUR SECONDS!? *WOW!*
THANK YOU, ADORING PUBLIC!
WELL, BELL. I'VE NEVER SEEN *ANYONE* STAY UP THAT LONG!
HA. YOU AIN'T SEEN NUTTIN' YET, *POTTS.*
HEY! DID HE JUST GIVE ME AN "S" FOR THAT?
A
PHYS. ED.
S
I AM SATISFACTORY!

sixteen

I CAN'T BELIEVE YOU STAYED UP THERE FOR SIXTY-FOUR SECONDS! YOU'LL HAVE TO TELL DAD ABOUT THAT WHEN HE GETS BACK FROM HIS TRIP!
I WILL—HEY, LOOK! HE'S BACK ALREADY!
WELL, HI, GEORGE! HOW WAS THE CONFERENCE?
YEAH, DAD! WHAT'DJA BRING ME?
AHHH...IT'S A GOOD ONE!
I EVEN WRAPPED IT!
MAYBE IT'S A NEW PHONIC EAR!

THE SUSPENSE IS KILLING ME!
WHOA! THAT'S NOT A PHONIC EAR— IT'S A PENCIL! A *CURLY* PENCIL!
GEE, DAD! A CURLY PENCIL! I'VE NEVER SEEN ANYTHING LIKE IT! IT'S *AWESOME!* THANKS, DAD!
GLAD YOU LIKE IT!
OH MAN! IT WRITES LIKE A REAL PENCIL, TOO! THAT IS *SO COOL!*
I do the rest of my homework with my new curly pencil, even though it takes a whole lot longer.
I CAN'T WAIT TO SHOW THIS TO EVERYBODY AT SCHOOL TOMORROW!

When I wake up the next morning, I don't have the usual sinking feeling that I've had every day since the Phonic Ear broke. Instead, I am excited!
BEHOLD!
I dress quickly...
GO, GO, GO!
...I eat quickly...
GO, GO, GO!
GOOD GRIEF!
...and I hurry out the door.
GO, GO, GO!
WAIT! DON'T FORGET YOUR LUNCH MONEY!
JUST WAIT TILL THE KIDS AT THE BUS STOP SEE THIS! MAYBE EVEN MARTHA WILL BE IMPRESSED!

Shoot. Martha's not here yet. But Mike is!
HEY! LOOK WHAT I GOT!
TA-DA!
WOW!
NEAT!
MY DAD GAVE THIS TO ME. YOU CAN HOLD IT, BUT BE CAREFUL! IT COULD BREAK, JUST LIKE A REAL PENCIL CAN!
CAREFUL!

GEE, THAT'S REALLY COOL!
NIFTY!
WOW! HERE YA GO, MIKE.
Even Mike Miller is impressed. *Swoon!*
THAT'S AMAZING!
HERE, JOHNNIE.
HUH?
THIS IS **STUPID**.

CRACK!
HERE YA GO. HAR HAR.
WHAT'D YOU DO THAT FOR?
I DUNNO.

SNIFFLE...
WAH!
I CAN'T BELIEVE THIS! I'M IN THE FIFTH GRADE AND I'M BAWLING IN FRONT OF EVERYBODY! IN FRONT OF MIKE MILLER!—AGAIN!
BWAH—WAH!
CECE?
UH...UH...
MAMA!

MAMAAAAAAA!
SLAM!
MY GOODNESS! WHAT HAPPENED?
JOHNNIE BROKE MY CURLY PENCIL ON PURPOSE! SO I'M THROWING IT AWAY!
THAT'S TERRIBLE! YOU CAN CERTAINLY STAY HOME TODAY, IF YOU WANT TO...
AND MISS SCHOOL? I CAN'T DO THAT!
WELL, ASHLEY AND SARAH CAN TAKE YOU ON THEIR WAY TO SCHOOL...
SNIFF!
HOW AM I GONNA FACE EVERYBODY NOW?

When I get to school, I go to the gym like always and sit in the bleachers. But no *way* am I sitting with the neighborhood kids—or any other kids, for that matter.
I stare straight ahead and try not to cry anymore.
But suddenly, out of the corner of my eye, I see somebody coming—it's *Johnnie*! And he's being pushed toward me by *MIKE MILLER*!
OK, JOHNNIE. *APOLOGIZE.*
UH, SORRY ABOUT THE PENCIL.
UH...

I DON'T KNOW *WHAT* TO FEEL...
UM, LISTEN. I'M SORRY ABOUT WHAT HAPPENED. IT WAS A REALLY COOL PENCIL. I DON'T KNOW WHY HE FELT LIKE HE HAD TO DO THAT!
...SHOULD I FEEL HAPPINESS, BECAUSE MIKE MILLER REALLY *IS* NICE AND MIGHT ACTUALLY CARE ABOUT ME?
UH...
OR *SHAME*, BECAUSE *MIKE MILLER* WITNESSED THE WHOLE THING...
UH...
WELL, I GOTTA GO...
...AND HE JUST FEELS *SORRY* FOR ME AND MY WHOLE *CRYBABY DEAF KID* SELF?
BYE. HOPE YOU FEEL BETTER.
AND NOW HE'S GONE. *MIKE MILLER* WAS SITTING RIGHT HERE BESIDE ME, AND I NEVER SAID A WORD! *RATS.*
BYE.

seventeen

The rest of that awful morning passes by in a blur.
MEH-EH SIN-A-MANN EZZ ETTS IME OR HIE-ETT MAAAAAAA...
HUH?
I SAID, MIS-SUS SINK-LE-MANN SAYS IT'S TIME FOR QUI-ET MATH!
OH. THANKS.
Quiet Math = we quietly do our math while Mrs. Sinklemann goes somewhere else for twenty minutes. I used to be able to hear where she went:
ZZZZZZZZZZZZZZZZ
SO THEN I SAID...
puff puff
AAAAHH...
tinkle tinkle
But not anymore.
YAWN!
NOT ONLY IS SCHOOL HARD WITHOUT THE PHONIC EAR, IT'S BORING, TOO!

Anyway, most of us work while Mrs. Sinklemann is gone...
...but sometimes, a few of us don't.
HEY, MIKE! CATCH!
WHOOP!
Sometimes the "bad" kids remember to watch the door for Mrs. Sinklemann.
GOD BLESS MY UNDERWEAR, THEY'RE THE O-NLY PAIR I HAVE! STAND BESIDE THEM, AND GUIDE THEM...
UH-OH...
But sometimes, like today, they forget.
SLAM!
CHILDREN! JUST WHAT IS GOING ON HERE? BACK TO YOUR SEATS— RIGHT NOW!
BETTER LOOK BUSY!

Uh-oh. Mrs. Sinklemann stands in front of her giant apple painted on the blackboard.
I AM SO DISAPPOINTED.
PAUL, J.P., MIKE, BECKY, MANDY— I'M WRITING YOUR NAMES IN THE APPLE...
Paul
Mike
J.P.
Mandy
Becky
...AND AS YOU KNOW, A FEW ROTTEN SPOTS SPOIL THE WHOLE THING. GOODNESS. LET'S PUT OUR THINGS AWAY AND GET READY FOR LUNCH.
MIKE SURE LOOKS EMBARRASSED. I WISH I COULD TALK TO HIM AND MAKE HIM FEEL BETTER. BUT HE PROBABLY THINKS I'M A BIG CRYBABY AFTER THIS MORNING.
UGH! JUST TALK, CECE!
UH...MIKE?
YEAH?

COME ON! TALK!
UH...
JUST SAY, "THANKS FOR WHAT YOU DID THIS MORNING"!
UH...
HANKS FOR WHAT YOU DID THIS MORNING THANKS FOR WHAT YOU DID THIS
ORNING THANKS FOR WHAT YOU DID THIS MORNING THANKS FOR WHAT YOU
ID THIS MORNING THANKS FOR WHAT YOU DID THIS MORNING THANKS FOR W
UH...
I'M READY TO EAT!
UM... YEAH.
"UM, YEAH"? PATHETIC! HOW CAN I EVER BE FRIENDS WITH HIM IF I CAN'T EVEN TALK TO HIM? RATS.

eighteen

Every day after school, I ask Mom the same question, and I get the same answer:
IS IT HERE YET?
NOT YET.
IS IT HERE YET?
NOT YET.
IS IT HERE YET?
NOT YET.
Until finally, after four weeks and three days of waiting...
IS IT—
YES!
OH BOY!
OH, MY PRECIOUS! HOW COULD I HAVE EVER BEEN ASHAMED OF YOU? LIFE HAS BEEN A MESS WITHOUT YOU AND THE MICROPHONE!

The next day at school, I am actually happy to be holding the microphone as I walk past everyone.
OH, IT'S BACK! HOW LOVELY!
TESTING, 1-2-3...
TESTING, 1-2-3...
CECE, CAN YOU HEAR ME A LITTL BETTER NOW?
YES!
TURN YOUR MATH BOOKS TO PAGE 153 FOR FRACTIONS
NOW THAT I CAN HEAR AND UNDERSTAND MRS. SINKLEMANN AGAIN, SCHOOL'S GONNA BE A *BREEZE*!

My day gets even better when Mrs. Sinklemann makes this announcement:
AS YOU MAY KNOW, THE SIXTH-GRADERS ARE GIVING A PRESENTATION CALLED "THE WONDERFUL WORLD OF BOOKS." IT'S A BIG PART OF OUR SCHOOL-WIDE "READING IS FUN" CAMPAIGN.
THE SIXTH-GRADE TEACHERS HAVE REQUESTED TWO FIFTH-GRADERS "ON THE SMALLISH SIDE" TO POSE AS GIANT BOOKENDS ON THE STAGE DURING THE PRESENTATION.
THE FIRST STUDENT I'VE SELECTED IS... CECE BELL!
REALLY!? I GET TO BE ON STAGE AND EVERYTHING? WOW!
AND THE SECOND STUDENT I'VE SELECTED—A BOY—IS...
A BOY?! MIKE IS KINDA SHORT. COULD IT BE?
MIKE MILLER!
IT IS!

CECE AND MIKE— I WILL LET YOUR MOMS KNOW...
...AS THEY'LL NEED TO GET YOU SOME MATCHING PAJAMAS.
HEE HEE HEE!
WHAT!? MATCHING PAJAMAS? IN FRONT OF THE WHOLE SCHOOL? AND NO WAY AM I "ON THE SMALLISH SIDE"!
I DON'T WANT TO WEAR PAJAMAS IN FRONT OF THE WHOLE SCHOOL, EITHER. HOWEVER... MIKE MILLER. IN PAJAMAS.
THIS COULD GET EMBARRASSING.

A few days later, after school...
WELL, HI! LISTEN, DON'T START YOUR HOMEWORK YET. WE'RE GOING TO THE MILLERS' HOUSE TO GET THE PAJAMAS THAT MRS. MILLER BOUGHT FOR YOU!
MIKE MILLER'S HOUSE?!
HI, NANCY!
COME ON IN!
OK. HERE ARE CECE'S PAJAMAS...
SO PRECIOUS!
RUFFLES?!
...AND HERE ARE MIKE'S PAJAMAS!
ADORABLE!
MOM!
ADORABLE...
UH, THOSE PAJAMAS ARE KINDA GOOFY, DON'T YOU THINK?
UH...YEAH...
I'LL LOOK GOOFY. HE'LL LOOK SO CUTE!

On the morning of the presentation, there's an announcement over the loudspeaker.
CLASS, WE'LL BE GOING TO THE GYM IN TWENTY MINUTES. MIKE AND CECE, YOU GO ON AHEAD...
THAT'S US. YOU READY?
"US"? OH YES!
We grab our pajamas and silently head to the restrooms to change. Well, *almost* silently. Thanks to the Phonic Ear, I can still hear Mrs. Sinklemann talking to our class.
CLASS...LET'S LINE UP
AND GET R
THE PRESE
REMEMBER
POLITE TO
SIXTH GR
BOYS
THIS IS NUTS.
GIRLS
UH...
WOW.

All the classes file in. The sixth-graders start singing. Mike and I sit. And sit. And sit. Suddenly, I hear something weird...
THE BLACK CAULDRON
The Secret Garden
MATILDA
Charlotte's Web
James and the Giant Peach
OOGA LOO MA GOOGA MOOO, AN LALA MA GA WAH...
THE Wonderful World OF BOOKS!
...and it ain't singing!
tinkle tinkle tinkle
AAAAAAAAAAAAAAAA...
SWEET RELIEF.
WOCKA WOCKA
HEE HEE!
FLUSH!
HA HA! SNORT!
I HAVE GOT TO STOP LAUGHING!

The presentation ends. The sixth-graders take a bow, and so do we.
I SEE MRS. SINKLEMANN HAS COME BACK. HOPE SHE HAD FUN IN THE POTTY! OH! I GOTTA STOP GIGGLING!
THE BLACK CAUL
The Secret Go
MATILD
Charlotte's
James and the Gia
CLAP CLAP
CLAP CLAP
A few minutes later, we change into our regular clothes and head back to class.
I HOPE I *NEVER* SEE THESE PAJAMAS AGAIN! LET'S JUST LEAVE THEM HERE IN THE BAGS.
UH...OK.
I HOPE I *DO* SEE THOSE PAJAMAS AGAIN!
SO...*UMM*. WHAT WERE YOU GIGGLING ABOUT UP THERE?
SHOULD I TELL HIM? I'VE NEVER TALKED TO *ANYONE* ABOUT THIS STUFF. AND I CAN'T EVEN *BEGIN* TO TALK TO *HIM*. I WISH I REALLY *DID* HAVE SUPERPOWERS! THEN IT WOULD ALL BE SO *EASY*!

AHEM!
CECE, GO AHEAD AND TELL HIM! TELL HIM WHAT YOU CAN DO!
I MIGHT BE THE ONE WITH SUPERPOWERS, BUT GUESS WHAT?
YOU DON'T NEED SUPERPOWERS TO SPEAK!
CECE?
SO COME ON! TELL HIM! TELL HIM THAT YOU HAVE AN AMAZING ABILITY!
ARR OO OH HAY?
I...I WILL!
I SAID, ARE YOU OK?
HEH HEH... JUST THINKING, I GUESS.

UM...UH...YOU ASKED WHAT I WAS GIGGLING ABOUT EARLIER. WELL... I HAVE AN AMAZING ABILITY!
HUH?
I AM FINALLY TALKING TO HIM!
YOU KNOW THAT MICROPHONE MRS. SINKLEMANN WEARS? AND—AHEM—THIS THING THAT I WEAR?
YEAH?
WELL, SOMEHOW THEY WORK TOGETHER TO HELP ME HEAR MRS. SINKLEMANN BETTER. AND THEY ARE SO POWERFUL...
...THAT I CAN HEAR MRS. SINKLEMANN WHEREVER SHE IS IN THE ENTIRE SCHOOL BUILDING!
NO WAY!
SO, DURING THE PRESENTATION... GUESS WHAT I HEARD?
WHAT?
I HEARD MRS. SINKLEMANN... PEEING!!!
FOR REAL?!

THAT IS JUST *SO COOL!* IT'S LIKE YOU HAVE *SUPERPOWERS* OR SOMETHING!
YEAH, KINDA. UM... WE'D BETTER GET BACK TO CLASS.
HE GETS IT!
HOW ABOUT YOU COME TO MY HOUSE AFTER SCHOOL TODAY? I WANT TO TRY SOMETHING...
YEAH!!!
I MEAN, UH, SURE. *AHEM.* YEAH!
COOL.
MY FIRST DATE!
THIS JUST GETS BETTER AND BETTER!

nineteen

EL DEAFO'S FIRST DATE
FOR YOU, MY DARLING, SWEET CHOCOLATES...
POUR MOI?
LOVE
...AND A SINGLE ROSE. ITS BEAUTY SHALL NE'ER SURPASS THAT OF THE ONE YOU WEAR UPON YOUR BREAST!
LOVE
DID HE JUST SAY "BREAST"?
NOW KISS ME!
LOVE
Smooch!
SEE YA SOON! AND WEAR THAT HEARING AID—BRING THE MICROPHONE, TOO!
HMM...THAT'S NOT QUITE WHAT I HAD IN MIND...

I take my school stuff home and then head right over to Mike's house.
HI!
HEY! OH, GOOD! YOU'VE GOT THE MICROPHONE!
I WANNA DO A LITTLE EXPERIMENT. *I'LL* WEAR THE MICROPHONE AND WALK DOWNTOWN. *YOU* STAY HERE. *I'LL* TALK THE WHOLE TIME, AND *YOU* CAN LISTEN. THEN WE'LL KNOW JUST HOW STRONG THIS THING REALLY IS!
WHAT D'YA THINK?
OK, I GUESS!
TESTING, TESTING, CA
YOU
EAR ME?
TESTING, CAN YOU HEAR ME?
YEP!
Mike heads downtown, and I listen.
KNOW YOU CAN PROBABLY STILL
I'M AT DAN'S HOUSE.
THIS IS A REALLY WEIRD "*DATE*"...
..NOW I'M CROSSING THE STREE
AT DAVID'S
HOUSE...TESTING, 1-2
BUT I'LL TAKE IT!

I keep listening...
......ARE YOU STILL THERE, CECE? NOW I'M IN FRONT O TRICIA'S HOUSE...I'M GONNA KEE ON GOING DOWNT
I GOTTA ADMIT, THIS IS PRETTY NEAT! EVEN I DIDN'T KNOW IT COULD GO THAT FAR!
Minutes pass. Then Suzie, a neighborhood kid, appears.
HEY, CECE! WHATCHA DOIN'?
SHOULD I TELL HER? I TOLD MIKE MILLER, AND HE WAS OK WITH IT...
I CAN TELL OTHER PEOPLE TOO—RIGHT?
I decide to take a chance. I explain the whole thing to Suzie. And she says:
SERIOUSLY?! THAT'S AMAZING! WHERE IS MIKE NOW?
...NOW I'M AT THE BIG BAPTIST CHURCH...AND
AT THE BIG BAPTIST CHURCH!
A few more minutes pass, and Suzie's friend Helen appears.
WHAT'S GOING ON?
GET THIS! MIKE IS WEARING CECE'S MICROPHONE THING AND HE'S WALKING DOWNTOWN AND TALKING, AND SHE CAN HEAR IT ALL!
WHAT'S HAPPENING?
IT'S SO COOL! CECE IS LISTENING TO MIKE...
WHERE IS HE NOW?
PAWN SHOP
THIS IS A LITTLE EMBARRASSING. BUT HECK! THEY THINK I'M COOL!
WHAT'S HE SAYING?

And then *another* kid shows up. But not just any kid—it's *Martha*!
WHAT'S EVERYBODY DOING?
MIKE'S USING CECE'S MICROPHONE THING AND HE'S TALKING TO HER WHILE HE WALKS DOWNTOWN!
SHE CAN HEAR EVERYTHING HE SAYS!
HE'S AT THE PAWN SHOP *RIGHT NOW!*
STICK AROUND! CECE'S BEEN TELLING US WHERE HE IS AND WHAT HE SAYS!
UH...
PLEASE STAY!
UMM...I GOTTA GO PICK UP SOME STUFF FOR MY MOM AT THE GREEN MARKET.
IT *DOES* KINDA SOUND LIKE FUN.
PLEASE STAY PLEASE STAY PLEASE STAY *PLEASE!*
BUT I GOTTA GO.
RATS...

WELL, WHAT DO YOU HEAR NOW?
JUST STATIC.
OH. WELL, I GUESS WE'LL GO PLAY SOME KICKBALL. LET US KNOW IF IT GETS INTERESTING AGAIN!
OK— BYE!
WHAT A STRANGE DAY! PAJAMAS AT SCHOOL. A "DATE" WITH MIKE MILLER. EVERYONE THINKS THE PHONIC EAR IS COOL. AND MARTHA DIDN'T TOTALLY AVOID ME...
AND NOW THERE'S SO MUCH STATIC! MIKE MUST HAVE GONE FARTHER THAN THE MICROPHONE CAN.
ZZZZCRACKLEZZZPOPZZZZ
IN FRONT OF THE DR
OH, HEY THERE!
WHATCHA DOING?
BUT WAIT! HE'S BACK! AND THE MICROPHONE IS PICKING UP ANOTHER VOICE!
HI, MIKE! I JUST GO
SOME THINGS FOR MY MOM.
ARE YOU TALKING TO CECE?
TRYING TO FIGURE
AR THIS THING CAN
DO YOU WANT
SAY SOMETHIN
HER?
IS THAT MARTHA!?
UH...I'D BETTER NOT.
HUH? WHY NOT?
COME ON, MARTHA! PLEASE SAY SOMETHING TO ME! ANYTHING!

I CAN'T TALK TO HER! YOU SEE, I HURT HER EYE LAST SUMMER, AND IT TOTALLY FREAKED ME OUT!
I MEAN, SHE ALREADY LOST HER HEARING, AND SHE'LL NEVER GET THAT BACK! I THOUGHT I HAD MADE HER BLIND, TOO!
BUT YOU DIDN'T!
I KNOW THAT NOW. BUT I WAS SO AFRAID OF HURTING HER AGAIN THAT I STAYED AWAY.
AND NOW I'VE STAYED AWAY SO LONG THAT SHE DOESN'T LIKE ME ANYMORE! I REALLY MISS HER...AND...AND...
...AND, OH! SHE'S RIGHT THERE, WAITING FOR YOU!

MARTHA! YOU *SILLY!* OF *COURSE* I STILL LIKE YOU!
I HEARD EVERYTHING YOU SAID! I DON'T *CARE* ABOUT MY EYE! I JUST WANT TO BE FRIENDS AGAIN. PLEASE? *PLEASE?!*
YOU *HEARD* ALL THAT!?
YES, I DID!
PLEASE, MARTHA? PLEASE SAY WE CAN BE FRIENDS AGAIN!
WOW.
UM...I'M GLAD YOU'RE NOT MAD. BUT— *OH!* I DON'T KNOW *WHAT* TO DO! AND MY MOM NEEDS HER STUFF! I GOTTA GO!
WAIT!

RATS. WELL, AT LEAST SHE *TALKED* TO ME FOR ONCE...
CECE?
UM, I DIDN'T REALLY BELIEVE YOU AT FIRST, BUT OUR EXPERIMENT PROVED IT! THIS THING IS *STRONG!*
YEP.
...AND HECK, *MIKE MILLER* IS TALKING TO ME *NOW!*
THAT WAS FUN! MAYBE WE CAN HAVE EVEN *MORE* FUN WITH IT AT SCHOOL!
FUN? WHAT KIND OF FUN?
I DUNNO. BUT I'LL THINK OF *SOMETHING!*
HMM. SOUNDS LIKE *TROUBLE.* AND I SURE DON'T WANT TO BE A ROTTEN SPOT ON MRS. SINKLEMANN'S APPLE!
BUT FOR *MIKE MILLER,* I'D DO ALMOST ANYTHING...
WELL— SEE YA!
...AFTER ALL, THANKS TO HIS "EXPERIMENT," THE NEIGHBORHOOD KIDS THINK I'M *COOL*...
...AND MARTHA SPOKE TO ME...
...AND—*GEE!* HE'S AN ABSOLUTE *DREAMBOAT!*
BYE!

twenty

The next morning on the bus, I save a seat for Martha.
I JUST *KNOW* I CAN CONVINCE HER TO BE FRIENDS AGAIN!
HEY, CECE! IS THIS SEAT TAKEN?
UH...
HOW CAN I SAY NO?
YOU KNOW WHAT I KEEP THINKING ABOUT?
ME?
YOUR HEARING AID AND THAT MICROPHONE! THEY'RE SO COOL!
COOL!? WOW! BUT DOES HE THINK *I'M* COOL, TOO?
SO...I'VE GOT A PLAN. WHEN MRS. SINKLEMANN LEAVES TODAY FOR QUIET MATH, YOU CAN USE YOUR STUFF TO LISTEN OUT FOR HER. WE CAN ALL HAVE FUN UNTIL YOU TELL US SHE'S COMING BACK! YOU'LL BE A *HERO*! WHAT D'YA SAY?
UM... SURE!

Once I'm at school, though, I'm not so sure about Mike's big plan. I can't concentrate on anything, not even on what Mrs. Sinklemann is saying.
WHAT HAVE I JUST AGREED TO DO? AND WHAT IF IT DOESN'T WORK? AND—OH!—WHAT IF I GET IN BIG TROUBLE?
MIKE AND THE NEIGHBORHOOD KIDS THINK MY HEARING AID IS COOL—BUT WHAT IF MY CLASSMATES DON'T THINK SO?
WILL I BE A HERO? OR WILL I BE HUMILIATED?
Suddenly, Mrs. Sinklemann's voice is all too clear:
CLASS, IT'S TIME TO PUT YOUR ART THINGS AWAY. QUIET MATH IS STARTING SOON!
BE GOOD, EVERYONE! I'LL BE BACK IN TWENTY MINUTES!
WHAT!? ALREADY?

I hear the tap of Mrs. Sinklemann's shoes as she goes up the stairs. Can I really do what Mike wants me to do?
TAP TAP TAP...
OK, EVERYBODY...
LET'S PARTY!
NO WAY! I DON'T WANNA BE A ROTTEN SPOT AGAIN!
ME, NEITHER!
DON'T WORRY! ME AND CECE HAVE A PLAN!
OH YEAH? WHAT IS IT?
CECE'S HEARING AID LETS HER HEAR MRS. SINKLEMANN WHEREVER SHE IS IN THE WHOLE BUILDING! SO CECE'S GONNA LISTEN OUT FOR HER AND TELL US WHEN SHE'S COMING BACK! WE CAN SNEAK BACK TO OUR DESKS—AND MRS. SINKLEMANN WILL NEVER HAVE TO KNOW!
OH BOY. WHAT'S EVERYBODY GONNA THINK OF ME NOW?

I wait for someone—anyone—to say something.
And then suddenly, someone does:
YOU CAN *DO* THAT?
WHERE IS SHE *RIGHT NOW?*
SHE'S IN THE TEACHERS' LOUNGE! I CAN HEAR HER PUFFING ON A CIGARETTE!
THIS PLAN IS *TOTALLY* GONNA WORK!
IT'S PARTY TIME!
BUT HURRY! WE'VE ONLY GOT ABOUT FIFTEEN MINUTES!

My classmates are having the time of their lives. I think about joining them, but I've got an important job to do. So I watch—and I listen.
I'LL GO INTO MY BUBBLE AND ACCESS MY ALL-POWERFUL EQUIPMENT THERE!

For the first time ever, El Deafo uses her superpowers for the good of others. By listening carefully, she cleverly deducts Mrs. Sinklemann's location at all times...
FUNNY—I MAY BE INSIDE THE BUBBLE OF LONELINESS...
SUBJECT: IN LOUNGE
...BUT IT'S NOT SO LONELY ANYMORE!
MS. BAUER, WOULD YOU MIMEOGRAPH THIS FOR ME?
SUBJECT: IN MA
N LOUNGE
IT'S ACTUALLY KIND OF FUN TO SHARE MY SUPERPOWERS—
HELLO, MR. POTTS.
EH?
BJECT: PASSING THRU GYM
AND JUST WAIT TILL THEY ALL FIND OUT THAT I CAN HEAR MRS. SINKLEMANN USING THE POTTY!
AAAAH... SWEET RELIEF...
• SUBJECT: IN BATHROOM • SU

Ten minutes later...
UM...CAN YOU STILL HEAR HER? I MEAN, LIKE, WHERE IS MRS. SINKLEMANN NOW?
WELL—AHEM—SHE'S IN THE BATHROOM!
NO WAY!!! THAT'S HILARIOUS! HEY, EVERYBODY! CECE CAN HEAR MRS. SINKLEMANN USING THE BATHROOM!
YOU CAN HEAR THAT? SERIOUSLY? THAT'S AWESOME!
GEE, I WISH I HAD A HEARING AID, TOO!
IT'S CRAZY! FOR SO LONG, I'VE WISHED THAT I COULD HEAR LIKE THEY DO. BUT I HAVE SOMETHING THEY DON'T HAVE—SUPERPOWERS! AND IT'S ACTUALLY FUN TO SHARE THEM LIKE THIS!
TAP TAP TAP...
BUT WAIT! WHERE IS MRS. SINKLEMANN NOW?

TAP
TAP
GOING DOWNSTAIRS
THIS CAN ONLY MEAN ONE THING: MRS. SINKLEMANN'S COMING BACK!
And now I have to warn my classmates that she's headed our way!
TIME IS RUNNING OUT! IT'S NOW OR NEVER! TELL THEM!
TAP TAP
But I never do stuff like this! I could get in so much trouble!
SO WHAT!? THIS IS YOUR PART OF THE PLAN!
TAP TAP
YOUR CLASSMATES NEED YOUR HELP. BE A HERO!
TAP TAP
STAND UP! SHOUT IT OUT! TELL THEM!

HEY, EVERYBODY! SHE'S COMING! GO BACK TO YOUR SEATS!

We get back to our seats just in time.
HOW LOVELY! I SEE THAT THERE ARE NO ROTTEN SPOTS FOR THE APPLE TODAY!
WE DID IT! I DID IT!

PSST! THAT WAS SO COOL! HOW COME YOU NEVER TOLD ME YOU COULD DO THAT?
UH...I DUNNO.
IS IT MY IMAGINATION, OR IS GINNY FINALLY TALKING TO ME IN A NORMAL WAY? THERE'S HOPE FOR US YET!
OH. WELL, IT'S NEAT!
UM, ANYWAY...MIKE TOLD ME TO TELL YOU THAT HE WAS RIGHT! YOU'RE A HERO!
OF COURSE I'M A HERO—
I AM EL DEAFO!

twenty-one

The next morning, during a brief recess before Quiet Math, we come up with a new plan.
I BROUGHT MY QUEEN RECORD! WE CAN PLAY IT TODAY DURING QUIET MATH! LIKE A *REAL* PARTY, WITH MUSIC!
I'LL LISTEN OUT FOR US AGAIN!
UH...GUYS? MRS. SINKLEMANN WANTS US OVER AT THE RUG...
We take our seats on the rug...
IT'S CRAZY! YESTERDAY I WAS SCARED TO DO THE PLAN. TODAY I'M *EXCITED!*
...and then Mrs. Sinklemann makes an announcement.
CLASS, WE'RE DOING SOMETHING SPECIAL TODAY. SO YOU'LL BE HAPPY TO HEAR THAT THIS MEANS THERE WILL BE NO QUIET MATH!
AWWWWWWWWWW!
MY GOODNESS! I HAD *NO IDEA* THAT YOU ALL ENJOY QUIET MATH SO MUCH! HOW *LOVELY!*

IT'S TIME FOR MORE OF OUR "READING IS FUN" CAMPAIGN! OUR GUIDANCE COUNSELOR, MRS. CATAWBA, IS GOING TO VISIT US THIS MORNING. SHE'LL BE SHARING HER FAVORITE BOOK WITH YOU—
—AND, OH! HERE SHE IS, RIGHT NOW!
HELLO, CHILDREN!
TODAY WE WILL BE READING FROM THIS WONDERFUL BOOK, *T.A. FOR TOTS*. IT DESCRIBES FEELINGS IN SUCH A CUTE WAY!
GROAN. I'VE SEEN THIS BOOK BEFORE. *SO* CORNY.
HERE'S HOW IT WORKS: IF SOMEONE SAYS SOMETHING NICE TO YOU, OR GIVES YOU A HUG, YOU FEEL GOOD, RIGHT? THAT FEELING IS A *WARM FUZZY*!
WARM
BUT THAT FEELING YOU GET WHEN SOMEONE IS MEAN TO YOU, OR HURTS YOU? THAT'S A *COLD PRICKLY*! *BRRRRRR!*
feelings
called
COLD

TODAY WE'LL BE MAKING OUR OWN WARM FUZZIES OUT OF POM-POM BALLS!
AND COLD PRICKLIES, TOO? I WANNA MAKE ONE OF *THOSE!*
GOODNESS, NO! NOW, GO BACK TO YOUR DESKS, AND I'LL PASS OUT THE MATERIALS...
Here's what we get:
Felt
pom-pom balls
GLUE
googly eyes
YOU'LL ALL BE GETTING ONE OF THESE PAPER BAGS, TOO. I WANT YOU TO PERSONALIZE IT. MAKE IT *YOU!*
ONCE YOU'VE MADE YOUR BAG AND SOME WARM FUZZIES, YOU'LL EXCHANGE FUZZIES WITH YOUR FRIENDS. YOU CAN KEEP YOUR FUZZIES IN YOUR BAG—AND YOU'LL FEEL GOOD ALL DAY!
STILL PRETTY CORNY—BUT AT LEAST WE GET TO *MAKE* SOMETHING!

I know *exactly* what to do with my bag. I get some yarn, some tape, and two old spools from the craft shelves...
WHAT A CRAZY COUPLE OF DAYS IT'S BEEN!
I FEEL SO DIFFERENT ABOUT A LOT OF THINGS...
...ABOUT MIKE, AND MARTHA... MY NEIGHBORS, AND MY CLASSMATES...
...I EVEN FEEL DIFFERENT ABOUT THE PHONIC EAR!
VOILÀ! THE PHONIC EAR BAG!
PHONIC EAR
AND ON THE BACK— A TOP SECRET PICTURE OF *ME!*
EL DEAFO

NOW—ON TO THE WARM FUZZIES!
VH
HEY, CECE! CHECK IT OUT! IT'S THE VAN HALEN LOGO!
GULP!
VAN HALEN!? THAT CRUMMY ROCK GROUP? WHAT HAPPENED TO HIM LIKING THE BEATLES? VAN HALEN? MAYBE WE'D BE BETTER OFF BEING JUST FRIENDS...
CHECK OUT THE BACK!
I'M CALLING 'EM WORM FUZZIES! GET IT? WORM?
HEE HEE!
WORM FUZZIES
THAT'S HILARIOUS! UM...HERE'S MINE.
IS THAT LIKE YOUR HEARING AID? THAT'S CRAZY FUNNY!
PHONIC EAR
WOW! HE GETS IT! MAYBE I'LL SHOW HIM MY DRAWING OF EL DEAFO LATER—BUT I'M NOT SURE ANYONE WOULD GET THAT...
WELL! BETTER START MAKING SOME WORMS!

I'M GONNA MAKE A LOT OF THESE THINGS, 'CAUSE I WANNA GIVE AWAY A LOT!
HEY, GINNY! CAN I USE YOUR SCISSORS?
GINNY
THIS ONE'S MY FAVORITE! MAYBE I'LL KEEP IT...
Twenty minutes later...
ALRIGHTY, EVERYONE! LEAVE YOUR BAGS ON YOUR DESKS, GRAB YOUR FUZZIES, AND START SHARING SOME GOOD FEELINGS!
Warm Fuzzies
I try to put a warm fuzzy in as many bags as I can.
GRAB YOUR FUZZIES? HEE HEE!
WORM FUZZIES
GINNY
And I make sure to put one in Ginny's bag...
SHE MAY BUG ME SOMETIMES...BUT SHE REALLY IS A GOOD FRIEND. I NEED TO BE NICER TO HER!
GINNY
...and in Mike's bag, too.
I HOPE NO ONE'S LOOKING!
WORM FUZZIES

BACK TO YOUR DESKS, EVERYONE! LOOK IN YOUR BAGS, AND ENJOY THE GOOD FEELINGS!
WOW! LOOK AT HOW MANY!
GINNY
AND—OH! A *WORM* FUZZY! I WAS HOPING I'D GET ONE!
PHONIC EAR
GINNY
CHILDREN, I MUST GO—BUT REMEMBER: YOU CAN REGIFT YOUR FUZZIES! SPREAD THE JOY!
REGIFT? I'M KEEPING *THIS* ONE—EVEN IF HE DOES LIKE VAN HALEN...

As corny as all that was, Mrs. Catawba was right. All those warm fuzzies make me feel really good...
CHIPS
...and the feeling gets me through the whole day. Even when I'm in P.E....
HI, MR. POTTS. CAREFUL!
I'M *TOTALLY* GONNA KICK THAT BALL TODAY...
...and *even* when I run into a certain person.
HEY, LAURA—LONG TIME NO SEE. WANT A WARM FUZZY?
HUH?
I pass out fuzzies on the bus ride home...
I'VE GOT SO MANY FUZZIES TO SHARE! I CAN'T WAIT TO GIVE ONE TO MOM AND DAD AND ASHLEY AND SARAH. AND I THINK I'LL GIVE MY *FAVORITE* FUZZY TO—

—MARTHA! I'VE GOT SOMETHING FOR YOU!
REALLY? FOR ME?
IT'S A WARM FUZZY—MY BEST ONE!
UM...
I KNOW—IT'S KINDA CORNY—
IT'S ADORABLE, ACTUALLY. THANK YOU.
PHONIC EAR
UM...ARE YOU SURE YOU'RE NOT MAD AT ME ANYMORE?
MARTHA! I'VE NEVER BEEN MAD AT YOU!
PHONIC EAR
BUT IT WAS AWFUL WHEN YOU WEREN'T TALKING TO ME.
I KNOW.
IT'S JUST—I FELT SO BAD ABOUT YOUR EYE. WHAT IF I'D MADE YOU BLIND?
BUT YOU DIDN'T!

AND THEN AFTER A WHILE, I FELT LIKE YOU MUST HATE ME.
OH, MARTHA. I DON'T HATE YOU. NOT AT ALL!
I THINK WE SHOULD START OVER!
REALLY? BUT WHAT IF I DO SOMETHING STUPID AGAIN?
FIRST, YOU DIDN'T. SECOND, CHECK OUT THESE MUSCLES! I'M TOUGH!
—SNIFF!— HEE HEE!
ACTUALLY, I SORTA HAVE A SECRET. AND YOU ARE PART OF IT.
WHAT IS IT?
I'LL TELL YOU. FRIENDS?
FRIENDS!
PINKIE SWEAR?
PINKIE SWEAR!

OK. I THINK IT'S FINALLY TIME TO TELL YOU ALL ABOUT...
EL DEAFO!
WHO?

EL DEAFO! AND HER *TRUE FRIEND*—YOU.

A Note from the Author

People can become deaf in many different ways. Some are born deaf, to either deaf or hearing parents. Some are exposed to one big, loud noise, and they lose their hearing immediately. Some might be exposed to lots of noise over a long period of time, and they lose their hearing gradually. Some might get sick with some illness or another and lose their hearing as a result of the disease.

Each deaf person also has a different *amount* of deafness—how much he or she can hear without the assistance of a hearing aid or a cochlear implant. One can be mildly deaf, moderately deaf, severely deaf, or profoundly deaf.

But more important than how the hearing loss happened, or how much hearing loss a deaf person has, is what a deaf person might choose to do with his or her hearing loss. In other words, there are lots of different ways to be deaf. And there is no right or wrong way.

Some deaf people are members of what is known as the Deaf community, also known as Deaf culture. Members of the Deaf community view their deafness as a difference, but it's a *good* difference, not a disability. Deafness is a condition that doesn't need to be fixed. Those in the Deaf community might—or might not—use hearing aids and cochlear implants to amplify sounds and speech. Sign language is the preferred means of communication in the Deaf community; Deaf people might—or might not—choose (or be able) to speak orally.

Other deaf people, however, *do* want to "fix" their hearing loss. They amplify their residual hearing with the help of hearing aids or cochlear implants. They may speak and read lips, and may or may not supplement their speech with sign language. They might think of their deafness as a difference, and they might, either secretly or openly, think of it as a disability, too.

And, I am sure, there are plenty of deaf people who would read the descriptions above and not recognize themselves at all. I am an expert on no one's deafness but my own.

I myself am "severely to profoundly" deaf, the result of a brief illness when I was four years old. While I'm fascinated by Deaf culture, I have not, as yet, pursued a direct role in it. Since I could hear and speak before I got sick, my parents were able to make decisions for me that kept me mostly in the hearing world. Their choices, and the choices that I made for myself later, helped me become pretty comfortable there. But I wasn't always so comfortable.

El Deafo is based on my childhood (and on the secret nickname I really did give myself back then). It is in no way a representation of what all deaf people might experience. It's also important to note that while I was writing and drawing the book, I was more interested in capturing the specific feelings I had as a kid with hearing loss than in being 100 percent accurate with the details. Some of the characters in the book are exactly how I remember them; others are composites of more than one person. Some of the events in the book are in the right order; others got mixed up a bit. Some of the conversations are real; others, well, ain't. But the way I *felt* as a kid—that feeling is all true. I was a deaf kid surrounded by kids who could hear. I felt different, and in my mind, being different was *not* a good thing. I secretly, *and* openly, believed that my deafness, in making me so different, was a disability. And I was ashamed.

As I grew up, however, I made some positive discoveries about deafness and about myself. I'm no longer ashamed of being deaf, nor do I think of myself as someone with a disability. I've even developed a real appreciation for sign language. To the kid me, being deaf was a defining characteristic, one I tried to hide. Now it defines a smaller part of me, and I don't try to hide it—much. Today, I view my deafness as more of an occasional nuisance, and oddly enough, as a gift: I can turn off the sound of the world any time I want, and retreat into peaceful silence.

And being different? That turned out to be the best part of all. I found that with a little creativity, and a lot of dedication, any difference can be turned into something amazing. Our differences are our *superpowers.*

Acknowledgments

I wish there was enough room on these pages to acknowledge every friend, every family member, and every person who was nice to me at one point or another. If you are one of the above, consider yourself acknowledged, and heartily!

A lot of people helped me create and promote this book:

Susan Van Metre believed in *El Deafo* when it was just a typed outline on two pieces of paper. She guided the book through every stage, and became a true friend along the way.

College pal David Lasky brought the book to life with his expert coloring and masterful shadow making. David's pal Frank M. Young assisted him a bit with a few of the later chapters.

Chad W. Beckerman and Katie Fitch used their estimable superpowers to put together this beautiful book. Caitlin Keegan came up with the gorgeous cover design. Sara Corbett guided the interior in the initial stages and was one of the earliest fans of the book.

Jen Graham read and reread the book so many times to get the text just right.

Sheila Keenan and Charlie Kochman shared their comics expertise.

Laura Mihalick and Jason Wells helped spread the word about *El Deafo*.

Caryn Wiseman did many things behind the scenes with positive energy and a smile.

New friend T.W. read the afterword and offered suggestions to make it better.

Emily Hemphill patiently posed for reference photos wearing the Phonic Ear and my old overalls.

Superfriends Madelyn Rosenberg and Mary Crockett Hill provided encouragement, a little extra PR, and a lot of extra laughs.

Amazing book people Raina Telgemeier, Tony DiTerlizzi, R. J. Palacio, Laura Given, and Travis Jonker read *El Deafo* early on, blurbed it, and filled me with relief.

And a lot of people inspired the book:

Martha Chadwick, who continues to be a true friend and soul mate.

Mike Miller, who really was that nice to me.

Emma Knight, who is my oldest friend.

Several other childhood friends, who upon reading this book might recognize bits and pieces of themselves. They might also think that they have been grossly misrepresented by my kid memories. I purposely changed their names because I know I wasn't always fair to them, in childhood or in this book. I hope they forgive me.

The neighborhood kids on Broad Street, who included me in lots of fun and games.

My classmates at Fisher School, who probably have similar stories to tell, and our teacher, Dorn Scherer, a kind soul who taught us the basics of lip-reading.

My teachers at Academy Street School and G.W. Carver Elementary School, who happily wore my microphone and treated me like all their other students.

The folks at Phonic Ear, who created the "school aid" that gave me superpowers.

Audiologists Michael Ridenhour and Dick Hawkins, who outfitted me with my first hearing aids.

The doctors and nurses at MCV, who helped me get better.

Ashley and Sarah, who are outstanding siblings and possibly the funniest people I know.

Mom and Dad, who made all the tough decisions during what must have been a tricky time in their lives. I wish I had better words than "thank you" to express how grateful I am to both of you.

C and O, who bring me joy every day.

And Tom Angleberger, who is my truest friend of all.

Cece Bell has written and illustrated several books for children, including the Geisel Honor book *Rabbit & Robot: The Sleepover.* She lives in Virginia with her husband, Tom Angleberger.